Sky's

BRIDAL TRAIN

Margo Hansen

MARGO HANSEN

Sky's BRIDAL TRAIN

· A NEWLY WEDS SERIES ·

TATE PUBLISHING & *Enterprises*

Published by Tate Publishing & Enterprises, LLC
127 E. Trade Center Terrace | Mustang, Oklahoma 73064 USA
1.888.361.9473 | www.tatepublishing.com

Tate Publishing is committed to excellence in the publishing industry. The company reflects the philosophy established by the founders, based on Psalm 68:11,
"The Lord gave the word and great was the company of those who published it."

Book design copyright © 2011 by Tate Publishing, LLC. All rights reserved.
Cover design by Kellie Southerland
Interior design by Sarah Kirchen

Published in the United States of America

ISBN: 978-1-61777-050-0
1. Fiction / Christian / Romance
2. Fiction / Westerns
11.05.09

To Bruce, my husband and love of my life. My respect for you grows with each day. It is your encouragement and belief in me that made this book possible, which is why I dedicate it to you with my love.

Acknowledgments

This first book in a new series has been my secret for a long time, mainly because I was afraid to tell others in case my attempt didn't succeed. Because of that, I acknowledge the following:

To *my Lord and Savior, Jesus Christ*. To God be the glory and praise for any accomplishment. May the message of salvation by grace through faith be clearly understood in what I write.

To *Bruce*, who never doubted, never laughed at me, and never minded the time I spent writing. Thank you for reading everything I have written.

To *Megan* and *Brooke*, my lovely daughters, who were the first to critique my work. You don't realize how much your encouragement has meant to me. I hope your children enjoy this book by their grandma Margo.

To *Casey*, my son. Your enthusiasm for my accomplishments delights me. I pray your own artistic endeavors succeed as God wills.

To my parents, *Harlan* and *Marilyn Nygaard*. You raised me to love the LORD and pointed me in the right direction in life. I will always be thankful for your guidance and still look up to you today. Thanks, Mom and Dad.

To my in-laws, *Leo and Pat Hansen*. Dad isn't with us today, but I know he would have been pleased. Thanks, Mom Hansen, for believing I could do it.

And to some special friends who have gently pushed: *Karie, Vicki, Jennifer, Linda, Evi,* and *Jackie*. Thanks for your not-so-patient-at-times waiting for publication. Believe it or not, you motivated me.

And to the *Tate Publishing family*. Thank you for giving me this opportunity and for the excitement of seeing my work in print.

The Brides

SKY HOFFMAN	MIRANDA PORTER
MARTHA SCOTT	GRETCHEN O'DONNELL
GERTIE CURRAN	BRIDGET O'DONNELL
VIOLET BOOTHE	ISABELLE PRY
ANGELINA SHARP	BERTHA GALLEY
NOLA ANDERSON	JANET CONLY

The Men of Sand Creek

CLYDE MOORE	JONAS NOLAN
NED BOLTER	HARRY NOLAN
GEORGE SPENCER	DUKE TUNELLE
BERT DAVIES	EVAN TRENT
JASPER RIGGS	ROY HILL
GERALD NESSEL	TAYLOR GRAY

Prologue

London, England

It was the day after her mother's funeral that the baron sent for her. Deep in her grieving, Sky had barely given the man a thought, but now as she nervously prepared for their meeting, she wondered what was in store for her. Her black dress contrasted sharply with her blonde hair and pale face. Her sky-blue eyes were dulled, and circles darkened the skin around them. Her head throbbed from her nightly sobs, and all she really wanted was to sleep so that she could forget that her mother was gone. Now she was alone.

The baron was not her father and had never liked her. Never given her any notice at all, in fact, other than to send her off to boarding schools whenever he could arrange it. Her mother protested and won her way a few times, but she knew only how far she could push the man and no further.

Even so, Sky knew she couldn't complain. She had a good life, a beautiful home, and a mother who loved her. But the distance between her and the man who was her stepfather was so great that she now wondered what he would do with her. At nineteen, she couldn't be shipped off to boarding schools any longer.

Penders waited beside the study door while she made her way toward him. The haughty butler was still annoyed with her, she knew, because of her directive that the household servants work as silently as possible so as not to disturb her mother. It seemed an unnecessary request, as common sense led most to react in sympathetic silence anyway, but Penders was not about to take orders from the baron's unwanted stepdaughter. So, following his employers's example, he ignored her too; and now he looked disdainfully down his long nose at her, his sight resting on her feet.

Her face crimsoned. During her mother's illness, Sky had taken to wearing slippers throughout the house to muffle her footsteps. Unfortunately, there had been the time when she was rushing to the kitchen for something for her mother, and Penders had stepped out of a doorway right in front of her. The shiny marble floor and the smooth slippers worked against her. Though she tried to stop, she couldn't and crashed right into the butler, causing him to spill the contents of the tea service down the front of him. Penders had barely kept his temper in check as he lifted his nose in the air and walked away from her.

How long ago that seems, thought Sky as her feet, clad this time in proper shoes, made tapping sounds as she crossed the marble entry. An empty sound in an empty house. Empty now without her dear mother.

At the proper moment the butler opened the door and announced, "Miss Hoffman, my Lord."

Wonder if he knows how big his nostrils look with his head tilted that way. Sky nearly stumbled in surprise that a humorous thought could possibly enter her grief-numbed brain of so many days, then quickly she righted herself as the door clicked shut behind her and she saw the stern man seated at the desk in front of her.

The baron didn't bother to stand at her entrance, just motioned for her to sit. Sky frowned slightly. Though cold to her, the baron had always shown the courtesy of rising when she entered a room. Wait. He only did when she was with her mother. And as Sky would never approach him without her mother, she had no way of knowing if this mannerism was new to him or not. Regardless, for a baron it was extremely rude and surely meant to indicate her status in his household. She tried to swallow but found her throat too dry.

Sky didn't twist her hands in her lap. She didn't hang her head. Her mother had always taught her to stand up for herself, and so now she kept her eyes on the baron and waited. She realized, belatedly, that this discussion would be about her future and that she should have come prepared with some options to offer, but her mind hadn't been able to cope with anything more than getting through each day up to the funeral. Now she found herself seated in front of the man who had control of what would happen to her. She had no illusions that it included staying in his presence. But she still wasn't prepared for his words.

"You are not my daughter." The baron pinned her down with his words and his icy stare. "Therefore, you will not inherit anything from me, and since your mother's death you are no longer my responsibility. Arrangements have been made for you. Be prepared to leave in two days' time. That is all."

Sky's voice was pinched from the dryness in her throat. "Arrangements?"

"That is all!"

The door opened at the baron's last words, and Penders, ramrod stiff, nose to the ceiling, waited beside it.

Sky rose slowly. As she stared at the unrelenting face of her stepfather, she understood that it would be the last time she would be in this room and the last time she would ever acknowledge him in any parental way. An oppressive weight seemed to roll from her mind.

With all the dignity her mother instilled in her, Sky walked from the room. She climbed the stairs, not really caring what the "arrangements" were. Later she would have time for that challenge, but for the moment she enjoyed a strange sort of freedom in no longer bearing any relationship to the man in the study. Penders's voice below caught her attention, and she paused on the landing as she heard the front entrance door being opened.

I can't bear any more sympathetic visits from the neighbors, she thought. Nevertheless, she steeled herself to descend the stairs again if Penders called her. She stared sightlessly at a painting on the wall before her while she waited. Behind her she heard male voices and recognized Penders as he announced the visitor to the baron. Then she stiffened and felt her skin tighten and prickle with the unpleasant feeling of being spied upon. She quickly swung around, but the man with Penders was just entering the study. As the butler was closing the door, she heard the stranger speak.

"Is that her?"

Puzzled, she stared at the door a moment, but Penders glared at her. She frowned, but as there seemed nothing more to do, she turned and continued her ascent up the stairs.

The next day, after a surprisingly restful sleep, the maids came with trunks and began packing her belongings, much as they had done through the years when she was sent off to boarding schools. Sky watched them in a detached manner, noticing that they didn't ask her any questions. Apparently they had strict instructions from the baron and were not about to disobey them.

Sky left them to their work and slipped quietly into her mother's room. As of yet, the baron hadn't removed any of her things, and it occurred to Sky that there were a few things her mother would have wanted her to have. With tears stinging her eyes, she took out the few pieces of jewelry they had discussed, leaving most items the baron had given her mother. *For all his coldness to me, he did love her.* Or at least he had some devotion to her as evidenced by the amount of jewelry resting on the velvet trays. She tucked the jewels into her pocket and headed back to her room.

A maid who had helped care for her mother called out to Sky in the hallway. Sky brushed back her tears as she turned and waited.

"Miss Hoffman." The maid was a little out of breath, and she cast furtive glances around as she approached Sky.

"Yes?"

"I haven't had a chance to speak with you since your mother...since the funeral and all." The woman seemed agitated as if not sure what to do or say next. Sky remembered that she hadn't been on staff long, in fact, had probably been hired mainly because of her mother's illness.

"It's Margaret, isn't it?" Sky tried to put the middle-aged woman at ease.

"Yes, miss." Again Margaret looked around, and then she pulled an envelope out of her pocket and pressed it quickly into Sky's hands.

"The missus, she said if something was to happen to her that I was to give you this here letter, miss. She said I wasn't to let the other maids know and certainly not the master." Margaret looked nervously over her shoulder as she whispered the words.

"I don't want no trouble, miss, or they won't keep me on, but I can't refuse a dying woman's request." With that she scurried off down the hall and out of sight.

Sky slid the precious envelope into her pocket but kept it tightly clenched in her hand. What had her mother needed to hide from the baron? She well understood why her mother chose to entrust it to the new maid, someone not yet under the baron's rule who would have shown it immediately to him instead of giving it to Sky. Suddenly

Sky needed to get out of the house and away from servants who did not serve her needs but those of the man who had disowned her.

She found her quiet spot in the garden and waited until she was sure there was no one around. There was still a chill in the air, and she shivered, wishing she had brought her shawl. The bench upon which she sat was icy cold, and without the green lushness and colorful flowers, the garden had an empty, desolate feeling, much like her heart. But none of that mattered when she was burning with an intense longing to see what words her mother had been compelled to leave with her. Words that were for no one but her to see. She glanced one more time at the imposing house. No windows for anyone to spy on her.

She took out the letter. Tears sprang immediately to her eyes upon seeing her mother's handwriting. So neat, so properly done, weak as she was from her illness. The usually strong penmanship revealed her frailty in the thin lines, only a light pressure used with each stroke. Sky took a deep breath.

"My Dear Sky—"

Suddenly a cry from the house caused Sky to jump up, shoving the letter back in her pocket. The maid Margaret rounded the corner, nearly running into her.

"Oh, miss! It's dreadful! There's been an accident!" She was out of breath and gasping.

"The baron, miss. He's dead!"

Chapter 1

Atlantic Ocean

The others would be going below soon. Sky hated to leave the fresh sea air and wind, but she knew she should not remain on deck alone. Breathing deeply one more time, she squinted into the setting sun ahead of her then turned to follow the other passengers, only to find her way blocked.

"Miss Hoffman, I do believe you've been avoiding me again."

How did he always find her? It seemed wherever she went on the ship, he was always close by, and she was getting very tired inventing excuses to avoid him. Anxiously Sky watched the retreating backs of her traveling companions while she warily eyed the tall English gentleman. Every time he was near her she was filled with apprehension. She forced herself to speak politely.

"Excuse me, Mr. Hadley; I need to check on Mrs. Lowe in my cabin." Sky moved to pass him, but his hand flashed out and caught her arm. She gasped at his boldness.

"But Miss Hoffman, the sun hasn't set, and you still haven't given me that stroll around the deck I've requested." He began to pull her along with him. "We have so much—Ow!"

Hadley jerked his hand away, and Sky could see red droplets pool on his wrist. He looked up in time to see her slide a hat pin into the corner of her shawl. His face darkened in anger.

"Was that really necessary, Miss Hoffman?" Rudolph Hadley spoke the words through clenched teeth.

"It was to me, Mr. Hadley." Sky spoke each word distinctly. Her heart was pounding while her blue eyes blazed at the man. She stepped forward to move around him, but once again Hadley blocked her path, though he avoided touching her. His eyes were hard despite his polite demeanor and silky tone.

"Our voyage is almost over, and you haven't given me any opportunity to get to know you better. But I *will* know you." His voice was almost a whisper in her ear. "Be assured I will have my opportunity."

Though his words chilled her, Sky spoke without hesitation. "Mr. Hadley, I have little patience left. Please let me pass, or I shall be forced to prick you again." Sparks fairly flew from her eyes, and as she spoke her hand went to her shawl.

"Be there anything I could be helping you with, Miss Hoffman?" Skip O'Rourke, one of the ship's crew, crossed over to her. His eyes darted to Hadley with a look of disdain then swung them back to Sky's in reassurance.

"Yes, thank you, Mr. O'Rourke." Relieved, Sky quickly sidestepped Hadley and tucked her hand into the arm the seaman offered her. "Would you please escort me to my cabin? I fear Mrs. Lowe will be concerned by my delay."

Sky clutched O'Rourke's arm and steeled herself to walk normally. She could feel Hadley's eyes follow her as she left the deck.

"There, lass, ye can relax a bit now." O'Rourke gave a fatherly pat to the trembling hand on his arm. His weathered face and short stature gave him a gnomelike appearance, but to Sky he was her knight in shining armor. "The captain told me to keep an eye out for ye. 'That Hadley fellow is up to no good,' says he. 'You see to it that he stays away from that pretty Miss Sky, O'Rourke.'"

Sky smiled at the old seaman.

"There now, lass, that's what I be meaning. That smile of yours fair stirs this old heart." He swooped his hat over his chest and sighed deeply. His expression was so comical that Sky could not help but laugh.

They reached her cabin, and she turned to face the kind man. "Thank you for helping me, Mr. O'Rourke. You are an angel."

"Oh now, lass, you'll be putting a halo on me head next. I best be getting back to me duties. Sleep well; I'll keep an eye out for ye." He gave her a quick wink before he walked away. As Sky turned to open her cabin door, she glimpsed the tall form of Hadley approaching. In a swish of skirts she entered the room, closed the door, and bolted it.

Mrs. Lowe, her cabinmate, was preparing for bed, her nightcap firmly in place. "What is it?" she asked in alarm.

"Shhh," Sky motioned to her. She placed an ear on the door and heard a faint chuckle then the sound of footsteps retreating down the passageway.

Chapter 2

Atlantic Ocean

"You've had trouble with that Hadley fellow again, haven't you, dear?" Mrs. Lowe whispered nervously.

Sky moved away from the door and acknowledged her plump traveling companion's question with a nod. Mrs. Lowe went on, "I heard him the other day boasting to some of the passengers about his large estates in England. He seems to be quite wealthy. He says he's just taking a pleasure trip to see America and maybe buy land—What is it, dear?" Genuine concern creased the older woman's face as she watched frustration cross Sky's.

Sky slumped down on the lower bunk, her head in her hands. "Why won't that man leave me alone? It's been like this ever since he discovered I was on this ship. He follows me and tries to start a conversation. He says we should 'get to know each other better.' I have no wish to know him at all! He presumes too much! I've even resorted to carrying a weapon." She indicated the long pin, which produced a gasp from Mrs. Lowe. "I don't care how wealthy he is or even if he is titled. He frightens me." She shuddered.

"He has a reputation of sorts in England, you know," Sky continued as she moved over to allow Mrs. Lowe to sit beside her, the tiny confines of the cabin allowing little room beside the bunks for the two women. "A girl at one of my schools told me about him. It seems he looks for a wealthy woman, usually a widow, and he woos her with his good looks and charm. Then he convinces her to marry him, and not long after the marriage she mysteriously dies, and all her wealth becomes his."

Mrs. Lowe's hand flew to her mouth. "And...you?"

"That's what I don't understand. I'm not wealthy. I have no idea why he is so interested in me. This girl said he has been under suspicion because it seems that his wives—and there have been more than one—have died from one sort of accident or another; none seemed to have been of natural causes." Sky shuddered again.

"Has he ever bothered you before?"

"No, I've never even seen him before this trip, only heard of him. Don't worry; I'll keep out of his way. Besides, I have enough to think about right now without having him to worry about."

"Your uncle's job offer?"

"Yes, he's paid for my trip back to America on the condition that I will work for him and his new wife in their tailor shop."

"*Back* to America, dear? You never told me that you've been there before," said Mrs. Lowe.

Sky noticed Mrs. Lowe's interest. She had been reluctant to tell her cabinmate much about herself during their voyage, but now she felt the need to confide in someone, so quietly she began.

"I was actually born in America. My father died before I was born; he was thrown by his horse and killed, and my mother left for England shortly after my birth, taking me with her. She married again, this time to a wealthy baron. I was raised in a fine home with many nice things, but the baron never really accepted me since I wasn't his. I often felt that my mother was sad because of this."

Sky paused then reached for the small bag beside the bed. She pulled out an envelope and from that a letter. Then she stood and paced the tiny cabin, pleating the letter in her hands.

"My mother came down with pneumonia and died, and shortly after her death the baron died in a hunting accident." Sky felt tears at the memory of her mother, so she cleared her throat and tried to gain control as she continued. "Before she died, my mother kept saying she was sorry. I didn't understand. I thought she was apologizing for the way the baron treated me.

"The baron's solicitor handled the legal matters. The baron left all his money to his brother who now bears the title. He left me nothing at all."

Sky heard Mrs. Lowe mutter something, but she didn't stop.

"At first I thought *that* was what my mother was sorry about. That she knew the baron had not included me in his will. But this letter explains the real reason." She handed the wrinkled paper to Mrs. Lowe.

My Dear Sky,

When you read this, I will be gone. I wish I could have had the courage to tell you this in person and answer all the questions I know you will have.

I love you very much. When you were born, I looked into your bright blue eyes so much like your father's, and I named you Sky. I always told your father that his eyes reminded me of the bluest skies. He would have loved you.

After your father's death, I was poor. I had no way to earn money, and I was expecting you. My sister and her husband took me in, but not out of the goodness of their hearts. Elaine was always jealous of me because your father married me, not her.

She arranged for me to marry the baron. He and I had met many years before, and he had wanted to marry me then, but I had eyes only for your father.

Elaine is not a nice person. She wrote the baron explaining about the baby and demanded money not only for our passage but also a fee for herself for her trouble. The baron still wanted me, so he reluctantly agreed to my bringing you. Sky, I had to agree to all this. There was no other solution that I could see. My only other hope of caring for you was through my brother, Peter, but he was off in the West somewhere at the time, and we didn't even know if he was alive, although now I know him to be in New York.

Now for the hard part, my dear. The night I gave birth to you, I gave birth to another baby as well. I had twins! The birthing exhausted me, and I slept soon after, but I remember the midwife put a baby in each of my arms and praised me for such 'fine looking wee babes.' I was happy, and I thought how proud your father would have been!

The next morning Elaine woke me and brought you to me. "Where is my other baby?" I asked.

She looked at me long and hard and said, "There is no other baby, Lucille. I had enough trouble getting the baron to agree to one; there is no more."

"What have you done with my baby?" I cried. She never told me. I pleaded with her for days, and then finally I refused to speak to her at all. A month later I left.

Elaine's husband, John, brought me to the ship. He was never as cruel as Elaine, so I asked him one more time if he knew what Elaine had done with my other baby. He didn't want to tell me, but finally he said, "She had the midwife take the baby to a family that was headed west by wagon train the next day. They had lost their own baby recently and were grateful."

So, Sky, my darling, you have a twin in America, somewhere in that western land. I barely saw her, but I have never forgotten her. I have tried to love you double to make up for you not having your father or your sister.

Find her if you can. I'm so sorry that I wasn't able to make it possible for you. Beware of Elaine. It would be better to avoid asking her help at all. I have never forgiven her.

Please forgive me for being so weak. Remember me with kindness.

All my love,
Mother

Mrs. Lowe folded the papers carefully and then looked up at Sky, who was staring out the small porthole. "Sky, you don't really expect to find your twin after twenty years, do you? America is such a large place. They say that a man can hide out in that West and never be found if he wishes it so." She paused and then reluctantly said, "Besides, dear, a newborn baby on a wagon train would have little chance of survival, don't you think?"

"I don't know!" Sky blurted. "But don't you see? I have to find out! All I know is that I must try, for Mother, and for me. If my twin sister is there, I'll find her." Sky squared her shoulders and continued to stare out into the night. "I must."

Chapter 3

New York

The voyage was finally over. Aboard the ship there was mayhem as passengers scurried for their baggage and jostled one another for a better view of the harbor. The ship's crew were running here and there, doing all the things necessary for landing and unloading.

In her cabin, Sky sat impatiently on her bunk, ready to go but not able to leave her cabin. Hadley's unwelcome attentions had imprisoned her there, preventing her from the excitement of finally arriving at her destination and getting a first glimpse of New York Harbor and her future. Mrs. Lowe had already gone up on deck, and her tearful good-bye had moved Sky.

"I'll be praying for you, dear. What you've set for yourself to do seems impossible to me, but if the good LORD wishes it to be, it will be."

Sky puzzled over that. Did God help people in situations like hers? She didn't think about God much. Her mother had once said that God doesn't care what happens to people. Sky could understand her mother's feelings, considering all that had happened to her. Her thoughts were interrupted by a knock.

"Who is it?" She rose and put her ear to the door.

"It's O'Rourke, lass."

Sky thankfully opened the door for her protector.

"I've got your trunks sent off to that address ye give me, and the boys are detaining Hadley in his cabin on the excuse that the captain needs to speak with him. If we go now, ye should miss seeing the scoundrel altogether. He'll have no way of knowing where ye went in this big city." O'Rourke grinned at his cleverness.

"Mr. O'Rourke, you deserve to wear that halo." Sky impulsively hugged the sailor.

"Now, now, enough of that." The surprised old man reddened then said, "Ye must hurry though, lass. I don't know how long we can keep him."

Sky grabbed her handbag and small valise and followed O'Rourke to the deck. He led her down the gangplank and into a carriage waiting close by.

O'Rourke looked into Sky's eyes, sighed deeply, then said, "Miss Sky, ye must be careful. The boys overheard Hadley tell his butler man...ye know, that thin, little man with the beady eyes?"

Sky nodded. Hadley's "gentleman's gentleman," Smythe, was a dangerous-looking man. He, too, made her feel uneasy.

O'Rourke continued, "Well, the boys heard Hadley tell that feller that he planned to marry ye and take ye back to England with him."

Though suspicious that Hadley was thinking exactly that, Sky was still alarmed to have the words actually spoken. She shook her head vigorously. "No, that will never happen!"

O'Rourke looked worried. "He has money, lass, lots of it. Sometimes that gives people power to do whatever they be wishing."

Sky appreciated the concern in the older man's eyes. "I will be careful," she said as she squeezed his hand.

"Bless ye, lass," he whispered, then he called out the directions to the driver, and she was off.

The carriage made slow progress at first as drivers yelled at one another and people scurried out of each other's way. But Sky was too intent on reaching her destination to really notice the busy city around her. Near the harbor was the worst, and the smells and commotion could have been overwhelming, but all Sky could think about was how she had come to be there.

London, England (one month earlier)

"If everyone is present, we shall begin." The baron's solicitor—a man small in stature but curiously imposing—peered at each person through wizened eyes behind wire-rimmed spectacles. He smartly snapped his papers together by tapping them on the desk then began reading the baron's will.

Sky heard the man's voice as if he spoke from a great distance. Her mind, benumbed by the events of the past weeks, prevented her from absorbing anything new.

She couldn't.

Her thoughts were too full of her mother's last letter to her and what she had to do.

A sister. A twin sister! An uncle. There was even an aunt whom Mother warned her against contacting. It was all astounding to her to find that she had some family left in the world.

The baron's death had thrown the household into turmoil and left Sky little time for her own affairs. Investigations were done, and she and all the staff had been questioned by the authorities until foul play was finally ruled out and accidental death was registered as the official cause of the baron's death. The baron apparently had stumbled getting off his horse, and his pistol had somehow discharged, killing him instantly.

The staff hesitantly turned to Sky for direction. It would have been funny under different circumstances to see how chameleonlike they really were. The baron had shown no regard for Sky, so the servants had likewise no respect for her, evident in the lack of actual service she received. Now with the baron and her mother gone, they assumed Sky was in charge and began kowtowing, referring to her as "my lady" and visibly trying to get in her good graces. Only Penders and a few he no doubt confided in held back their allegiance to her. Sky felt sure Penders had listened at the study door the day the baron informed her she would inherit nothing from him.

Which made it seem unnecessary for her to be here now, sitting in the study, the very same room where she heard those words, listening to the reading of the baron's will. Sky smoothed a wrinkle from her black dress and gave her head a little shake. She really must pay attention.

The only other occupants of the room besides the solicitor and Sky were Penders, the housekeeper, the cook, and the baron's brother. Sky glanced to her left to see the new baron standing off to the other side as if he wanted to watch the reactions of the others in the room.

Her stepuncle was a stranger to her. Oh, she had seen him on a couple of occasions when he arrived to visit the baron. As a little girl she had peeked into the parlor where the three adults—the baron, her mother, and the baron's brother—sat having refreshments. Her mother had spotted her and motioned for her to move away from the door, knowing the baron's dislike for interruption. And Sky moved on, but she thought she saw an amused expression on the visitor's face when he caught her staring at him.

There was no amusement in that face now. Sky didn't look directly at the man but sensed more than anything his perusal of her and the others.

The solicitor read the allotments the baron had made for his head staff members. It was modest if not generous, and Penders's nose rose proportionally in response.

"The entirety of my estates, personal belongings, material goods..." the solicitor's voice droned on, "...I leave to my only surviving relative, my brother..."

There was a gasp from the cook, and the housekeeper swung around to look at Sky, but Penders's only reaction was a slight nod, letting the others see he was in the know.

At this point the new baron stepped forward. He directed his attention to the servants.

"The estate will be sold shortly, and the new owner requires a staff. You will have the option to be interviewed for positions and remain here if selected, or you may seek other positions. I will provide recommendations to any who require them. That is all."

Something in the way he spoke or moved resembled so closely what the baron was like that Sky couldn't help the sigh that escaped her.

The door closed on the three remaining, lending an atmosphere of privacy although Sky had no illusions but that Penders's ear was tight against the door. The new baron turned to the solicitor.

"There is no provision for my brother's daughter, then?"

The solicitor raised an eyebrow. "She is a stepdaughter, my Lord. No, there is nothing." Whether he thought this action fair or not he kept absent from his expression.

Sky's stepuncle turned back to her and folded his arms across his chest. "Well, my dear, what are we to do with you?"

Sky wasn't sure if his words were meant to be unkind, but she had had enough of people telling her what to do or making arrangements for her. She stood, causing the solicitor to rise also.

"I'm sorry for your loss, my Lord, I truly am. But please don't trouble yourself about me. I have made plans and expect to be gone from here by the end of the month, if that is satisfactory?"

She waited for his nod but forestalled his words with her own. "Thank you. I shall leave you to finish your business, then." She curtsied to the two men and swept out of the room, nearly colliding with Penders as she stepped into the hall.

Sky received a reply from her uncle Peter in New York and left England sooner than she had expected. She said good-bye to no one and held no regrets in leaving other than the severing of her last link with her mother.

New York

The carriage stopped in front of a small shop whose auspicious sign *Tailor* was the only advertisement the window boasted. Sky paid the driver, realizing as she did so that her handbag was lightened considerably of the money her uncle had sent her.

"Uncle Peter," she said softly as she approached the door to the shop, "I wonder what you're like, and I wonder if you'll be able to help me." Peter Brighten was her mother's older brother. Aside from her aunt Elaine and her twin, he was the only other relative she had. After failing in business out west, Peter returned to New York and set up his tailor business and had only recently married.

After her mother's death, Sky had sent letters to America in search of her uncle and hopefully his help. Finally one had reached him, and he had put forth his offer to have Sky come to New York.

Sky opened the door to the shop, causing a bell to tinkle. Fabrics, ties, jackets, and shirts were displayed on two large counters before her in a myriad of colors.

"The shop is closed!" announced a shrill voice from the back.

Sky looked for the person who spoke but could see no one. "Excuse me, please," she called. "Is Peter Brighten here?" She heard a thud as if something heavy had been dropped. A small, thin woman wearing a stiffly starched apron over an equally stiff black dress that rustled while she walked approached from the back of the shop. She had a hawklike nose and narrow eyes.

She looked Sky up and down sharply then asked, "Who are you and what do you want with Mr. Brighten?"

Sky was taken aback by the woman's brusque manner but responded as politely as she could. "My name is Sky Hoffman, and Peter Brighten is my uncle. Oh! Could you be Priscilla, my uncle's new wife?" She stepped forward, her hand outstretched.

Her thin lips turned into a scowl, the woman made no move toward her. "So he did send for you after all, did he? Well I told him not to. 'We don't need any extra help around here,' I told him. 'Costs enough money to run this place as it is,' I said. But did he listen to me? Oh, no! Well, now we have a devil of a problem," she hissed.

Puzzled, Sky set down her valise and asked, "If I could see my uncle, please, I'm sure he can explain—"

"No, he can't," the woman interrupted. "He died two weeks ago. Heart failure, the doctor said. I told him he was taking in too much, but would he listen to me? Oh, no, not him!"

"Dead?" Sky leaned her hand on the nearby counter. "But he sent for me; he paid my way." She continued almost in whisper, "He was going to answer my questions."

"*Paid* your way, did he?" Priscilla Brighten snatched at the words almost before Sky finished speaking them. "Well, you'll have to be paying that back, miss. I'm packing to go live with my sister, and I'm taking all that belongs to me."

"I have no money to pay you back." Sky bristled. "My uncle would not have demanded that of me." She really had no way of knowing this, but the woman got her ire up.

"He was going to have you work for him, wasn't he? He would have taken it out of your wages. I would have seen to that." Priscilla's thin face showed triumph. "I'll have that money when I leave here."

"How can I work to earn the money if you are leaving, Mrs. Brighten?" Sky then looked around her. "And where will I stay?"

"I've sold the shop to Mr. Harry Hascombe of Boston." Priscilla pulled her thin lips into a conspiring smile. "He gave me just the price I wanted too. Perhaps I can work this to my advantage. After all, he'll be needing help." She paused, eyeing Sky once again. Then her shrill voice announced, "Yes, that might work."

Sky's fine eyebrows drew together. "What might work?"

"Nothing you need concern yourself with, Miss Hoffman. Now, if I'm not mistaken, your trunks have arrived. Run out and have the man bring them into this room right over here in the back. I shall be going out for a while; you need not concern yourself with where." Taking off her stiff apron, she pulled on a cape, set a hat on her head, and marched out of the shop.

"You mean to tell me no one saw her leave the ship?" Hadley sternly questioned his man Smythe while he paced the floor of his hotel room, deep in thought.

"See if this backwoods country has such a thing as a detective agency. I want her found as quickly as possible."

"Yes, sir."

Rudolph Hadley continued to pace the room after his man left. Oh yes, he wanted Sky Hoffman found. He had seen her once at her home while visiting the baron on a business matter directly related to her. It hadn't been the right time yet, but that one glimpse had convinced him to go through with it. She was beautiful! He had made note to keep his eye on her.

The baron's "accidental" death had been his doing, of course, but when he learned that the baron had left Sky penniless, Hadley put aside thoughts of her to pursue a widow of some wealth. He grimaced. Unfortunately, the three women he had married were somewhat less than beautiful. In fact, it seemed wealth and beauty were not compatible; the wealthy women usually were not beautiful, and the beautiful women were usually not wealthy.

But unable to keep Sky out of his mind, he changed his focus to Sky's stepuncle, the baron's brother. Taking a chance, he had the man's will investigated. With no family of his own to whom he could leave his wealth, the new baron had decided to leave it all to his niece, Sky Hoffman, whom, he claimed, earned his respect with her independent attitude. It was a simple matter, really, for Hadley to bribe a member of the man's household staff to slip a little something into the baron's food. The resulting death was diagnosed as heart failure, and although the authorities were suspicious, there was no reason for them to turn their attention Hadley's way.

Sky had already left on the voyage to America before she could be contacted about her inheritance, and Hadley just barely made it to the ship before it sailed. Hadley wanted to make her his wife before she was informed so that the money would go directly to him as her husband.

Finally he would have the beauty along with the wealth. And Sky Hoffman was about to inherit more wealth than he had ever seen before. The only obstacle was Sky herself, but Hadley wasn't too worried. He had always gotten his way before, and he would again. He only needed to get her back on a ship with him. Once there she could be forced into the marriage.

Yes, he would get his way.

Chapter 4

New York Harbor

Russ Newly tilted his Stetson back on his head and squinted at the sparkling water in New York Harbor. His first time in the city and his first look at the Atlantic had him amazed at God's marvelous creation and disgusted at man's proclivity to deface it. The ships and boats and commotion at the docks overwhelmed him, and he longed for the quiet of the forest, but at the same time he stood awed at the vastness before him.

Reluctantly he turned away and resumed his vigil, watching the small boat being loaded with crates and barrels. Patience was vital in his job, and as he settled his hat back in place, he wondered how much longer he could ignore the impatience building within him to finally settle down and take on a different sort of life than he had for the last five years. The thrill of adventure and travel had landed him this job in the first place, but that thrill was waning. On his last visit home, his mother had questioned him about his future, and he knew her inquiries were leading to the inevitable reminder that she wished to have grandchildren someday.

Russ sighed. Who would want to share this nomadic life with him? Orders moved him from city to city, from state to state, so quickly that no wife or family would be able to put up with it or him for very long.

He felt more than saw the nod given by his partner. Time to move in. His hand checked the gun at his side as he moved forward to do his job.

New York

"Has it only been a week?" murmured Sky to herself. "It seems like forever." She sighed and turned from the window back to the work of pushing the needle in and out of the fabric across her lap.

Priscilla Brighten was gone, and she left with the money she had wanted too. While Sky had been getting settled in her room at the back of the shop, her new aunt had indentured her to Harry Hascombe, the shop's new owner, for the price of one passage from England to America plus carriage and baggage fare.

Sky was outraged, but there was little she could do. She needed to pay back her passage money, but she also knew she was going to need money of her own to search for her sister. This job was one place to start. She sighed again and shook her head. What kind of man must her uncle have been to marry a woman like that? A noise behind her made her turn.

Harry Hascombe entered the room. He was a small man who obviously wished he was taller. Sky secretly laughed at how he walked with his chest puffed out and his head high. She knew he raised his shoes with blocks concealed between the heel and sole. He paused beside her, presumably to look over her work, and let his hand drop to her shoulder. "Why is this collar taking you so long, Miss Hoffman?" he demanded.

Having become accustomed to the man's tactics, in one quick motion Sky slid from the chair, moving her arm as she did so that her needle scratched the back of Hascombe's hand. With a jerk he pulled away and glared at her.

"You will watch where you place your hand in the future, won't you, Mr. Hascombe?" Sky said, carefully controlling her anger. "These needles can be quite slippery."

Hascombe's face darkened, and his eyes narrowed. "I know your game, girl, and don't think you will always get away with it. You're my property; I paid for you, and I will see that you repay every cent." He stepped toward the door of the shop, his movements awkward because of the shoes. "See that your work is completed before I return."

The door closed behind him with a sharp click. Sky shakily sat down but did not resume work immediately. How could she get out of this mess? Hascombe wasn't so much a problem to her as he was simply a nuisance, but the longer she stayed here, the more difficult things were sure to become.

She brushed tendrils of hair away from her face; her long, blonde braid was pinned in a coil on the back of her head, but strands of hair had escaped. She was frustrated at being held in this place by lack of money. Her aunt had reluctantly given her what little information she had about her twin. Sky didn't know if Priscilla was simply bitter at her uncle for dying or if she was simply a bitter woman by nature, but it had taken all the pleading and prodding Sky possessed to get even that much out of her.

When Uncle Peter returned to New York after his failed business venture out west, he had gone to see Elaine and John. Somehow in a discussion he had learned about his sister Lucille's twins and what Elaine had done. The wagon train with Sky's twin sister on it hadn't gone way out west as Sky's mother had been told but had actually gone northwest to the state of Minnesota. Sky wasn't going to find anything by staying in New York; she needed to go to Minnesota. Even then, she didn't know quite how to handle her search, other than to hope that someone there might see a resemblance to her sister in her. It was very little, but it was all she had. She was just thankful to have her search narrowed down that much.

Money was the problem. She had no cash money of her own. The only wealth she possessed was her clothing. The baron hadn't wanted her to appear shabby to his friends, otherwise she doubted that he would have given her even those. She did still have her mother's diamond; the other jewelry she had taken she had already sold. Sky bit her lip gently. She was saving the diamond for when she was without any hope, something she knew could happen.

She thought of her mother's situation and how, because of poverty, she had been forced to marry the baron. Sky again shook her head. That was not going to happen to her!

Two days later, Hascombe sent Sky to purchase some buttons from a tailor across the city. Sky hadn't been out of the shop since she had arrived, and she anxiously started out on foot, refusing the carriage partly because she decided to keep the money Hascombe had given her for it rather than spend it and partly because the pleasure of striding along in the fresh air was such a joy.

Today she left her golden hair in a long braid down her back, and she could feel it swinging in time to her step. Her dress, even though she had chosen one of her plainer ones, was elegant in comparison to the ones worn by the other women in the neighborhood. She realized that her clothing didn't fit her station as seamstress, but there was no help for it. Children scampered in front of her as she walked along, then they broke into a full run, and she had to resist the temptation to do the same. The sun felt warm on her shoulders, and she smiled up at it as if to say thank you.

But then a shadow fell on her.

"Miss Hoffman, are you ready for that stroll now?" Rudolph Hadley's tall form filled her path, and she cried out in dismay at having been discovered. He firmly grasped her arm and pulled it into his own. Sky tried to pull free, but his grasp was too tight. "No hat today, Sky? No hat pin either, I presume. I do like to see your beautiful hair in the sunlight."

"What is it that you want of me?" Sky pulled Hadley to a stop and stomped her foot. They stood in the street eye to eye, toe to toe; Sky, beautiful in her fury, and Hadley, darkly handsome in his insolence.

He laughed, and she felt his stale, dry breath on her face. "It's simple, Sky. I want to get to know you, and I usually get what I want."

Sky was astonished by the audacity of the man. "I'm *not* interested in getting to know *you*! Please leave me alone!"

"Like I said, I usually get what I want."

Hadley increased his pressure on Sky's arm and began to pull her with him, but with a quick move Sky pinched a handful of his skin between her sharp fingernails. Hadley gripped her upper arm between strong fingers that made her gasp in pain. They struggled silently, neither willing to give in, until Hadley began to bend her arm, and her hold on him loosened. He quickly gained the advantage.

"Not quite as strong or clever as you thought, are you, Sky? I do like your spirit, though. Come along. I have a carriage waiting around the corner. Isn't it convenient that I've found you so easily when I thought the detectives I hired would have all the fun of looking for you."

"Stop!" Sky gritted her teeth. Tears of pain filled her eyes, but she blinked them away and looked quickly around her. This couldn't be happening! Hadley was practically pulling her along with him, and she was unable to stop him. She was even more dismayed to see Smythe step around the corner and start toward them.

They were both jerked to an abrupt halt by a strong, sun-browned hand on Hadley's shoulder. A tall, dark man wearing a Stetson blurred past Sky's vision. She felt herself fall as Hadley's grip loosened, but an arm snaked around her waist and caught her then stood her on her feet.

Hadley spun around to swing at the intruding stranger, but the tall man gripped Hadley's arm with fingers of steel. The Englishman sucked in a gasp of air.

Smythe stepped closer and started to reach in his breast pocket when the stranger drew a gun with his left hand.

"Hold it there, mister. Get your hand away from the coat and just put them both up in the air and keep them there."

Smythe's expression was evil, but he did what he was told.

The stranger spoke to Hadley. "I don't know where you come from, mister, but I can tell by those clothes that it's not from around here. 'Round here we treat our women with respect. Now I would like you to apologize to this lovely young lady, and then we'll see that you and your friend over there," his gun never wavered from Smythe, "get to that carriage of yours around the corner."

During this speech the stranger hadn't loosened his grip on Hadley's arm, and by this time Hadley was fairly purple in the face with rage and pain. Sky stood a little to one side, astonished at what was happening.

The stranger turned to look at her. "Did he hurt you much, ma'am?"

She looked up into the suntanned face. As her eyes met his, she smiled in relief. "A little, sir, but I am all right now, thank you."

He nodded, and Sky saw an appreciative gleam in his eyes as he held her look. Her heartbeat, which was still racing from her shocking encounter with Hadley, now stepped up its beat even more in response to his obvious interest. Looking back at Hadley, whose face was now turning white, the stranger said, "Now, mister, the lady and I are waiting for that apology."

Hadley gasped out in a strained voice, "Sorry...I'm sorry. Let go now! Unhand me!"

"Sorry, who?" the stranger insisted.

"Sorry, Miss Hoffman, sorry!" He struggled for air. "I apologized. Let me go!"

"Okay, come along to that carriage now. Miss Hoffman, if you'll wait right here, I'll be happy to escort—" He turned to look at her as he spoke, but Sky was hurrying down the street, her skirts flying, away from the men.

The stranger looked after her, regret in his eyes.

"She's not for you, cowboy," gasped Hadley. "She deserves what money can buy her, and I have money."

None too gently, the tall stranger pushed Hadley forward, motioning with his gun for Smythe to fall in step. "Maybe the lady should have a say about who she wants, mister, and I'd be willing to bet it isn't you. Now, stay away from Miss Hoffman or I won't be so gentle with you next time."

Hadley fell into the carriage at the stranger's shove, and Smythe stepped in after him, his look still menacing.

The driver, at the stranger's directions, swung the carriage around in the opposite direction Sky had taken.

Russ Newly looked down the street where Sky had disappeared. He lifted his hat and combed his fingers through his black hair. *Lord, when you're ready to send me a wife, make it one like her, would you?* He looked skyward and smiled then chuckled at his thoughts.

He placed his hat back on his head, walked to where his horse was tied, and mounted. He hated to leave the city now knowing the pretty young woman was in some kind of trouble from the English gent, but in his business he had to be where he was told, when he was told to be there.

Lord, she needs your help. I know nothing about her except that she's frightened and seems to be alone. She's dressed in mourning clothes, so I know she's had some sorrow recently. Protect her, Lord, and if she doesn't know you, I pray she learns of your love and grace toward her soon.

Russ turned his horse westward. *Miss Hoffman.* He'd remember her, though he was sure he'd never see her again.

Chapter 5

New York

"You're not serious!" Sky's shock rang out in her voice. "Mr. Hascombe, I agreed to work for you to pay off the passage money you paid my aunt. You have no right to transfer that debt to another!"

"On the contrary, Miss Hoffman," Hascombe smiled, "I have every right. It is *you* who have no rights."

The tailor shop was closed for the day. Sky was tired from the hours of work and in no mood for this conversation. *What is the man doing to me?* Since arriving in America her life had become so complicated. She rubbed her puckered brow.

Hascombe fingered the material before him on the counter. His face showed little regret as he continued, "I have been offered not only the return of your passage fare but a substantial 'bonus' as well if I transfer your indenture." He began to pace in his awkward shoes, making an odd clopping sound on the floor. "Your work in the shop has been quite satisfactory, and though I would like to keep you, temper and all..." he lifted a tendril of her hair, but at the flash of her blue eyes, let it drop, "...I simply cannot refuse such a generous offer."

"I will not be bought and sold like a slave!" Sky was outraged. "I believe your country just fought a war to free slaves, Mr. Hascombe. Again I say you have no right!" She stood and placed her hands on her slender hips.

"Some would say that war isn't over," said Hascombe smugly. "I know there are those in the South trying to build up a new army and try again. Can't say that I blame them."

"I have been well instructed in America's affairs," Sky continued. "My mother saw to that. I know the law in this city would not allow you to *sell* me as you plan. I owe my passage fare, sir, and that is all."

Hascombe looked uncomfortable and unsure of himself as he cleared his throat and ran a finger inside his collar. Sky could see the conflict between truth and greed cross his features, and the greed won out.

He puffed himself up to his full, shortened height and commanded, "You will be ready by morning. The gentleman would not like to be kept waiting."

Suspicion filled Sky. "Would this 'gentleman' happen to be Rudolph Hadley of England?"

Something flickered in Hascombe's eyes at the name, but he merely replied, "The name matters little to you. As I said, you must be ready in the morning." With that he put on his tall hat and left the shop for the night.

"Oh, I'll be ready all right," muttered Sky. "This time I'll be ready, Mr. Rudolph Hadley." She quietly paced the room, deep in thought. Her lithe form had an animal grace in its movements, and her long hair swung from its ribbons with each turn.

Then she stopped abruptly and stood perfectly still. All was quiet but for the ticking of the clock on the wall.

"Now's the time," she whispered.

Train

The train rumbled and rattled and screeched as it made its way over the rails. Sky squirmed and changed position on the hard seat. She was tired. She'd had very little sleep the night before with so much she had to do. Fortunately she had unpacked only one trunk in New York, so it didn't take long to re-pack.

She had thought of selling some of her clothing but couldn't bring herself to do it yet. She and her mother had sewn most of the lovely garments. Others had been made for her by seamstresses according to her mother's instructions. They were her only real link to her mother's memory, and she couldn't part with them.

Her mother's diamond was different. To Sky, its memory was not a happy one, for it linked her mother to the baron.

The clacking of the train on the track was hypnotizing her, and her head nodded. A baby's cry startled her back to wakefulness with a snap of her neck, and she groaned as she rubbed the spot. Dust and the smell of coal filled her nostrils.

I wonder what Hascombe thought when he found my note and the money to pay off my indenture, thought Sky. *He's probably disappointed he didn't get that bonus.*

Sky packed soon after Hascombe left her in the shop. She slept a little then rose and went to a shop she had seen on the day she bought buttons. She woke the disgruntled owner and bargained with him on the sale of her mother's diamond.

Not totally satisfied with the amount she received, she nevertheless hurried on to her other errands. She had little time—train fare, baggage handling, repayment of her debt to Hascombe—she still had enough money to last her for a while, she calculated.

She'd hurried to leave the shop before Hascombe came for the day. Then she hid at the train station until her train left.

Only now did she feel safe and able to relax. In fact, she felt excitement tingle inside her. She was finally free to find her sister.

Three days later, Sky stepped out of the train for the last time. She was exhausted. She just kept paying the conductor to continue on down the line each time he requested her destination, and finally she could go no farther.

She looked around her at the dusty town. She didn't even remember what town the conductor said this was; all she knew was that she wasn't in Minnesota yet and that she couldn't ride another second on that train. Her sky-blue eyes felt dry and scratchy; dark circles emphasized their weariness. She stood slightly swaying on the platform, wondering what to do next.

A man in faded overalls and a train man's flat cap stepped over to her. "Welcome to Leaf River, ma'am. Will you need help with them trunks?"

Sky studied the man curiously. He wasn't exactly the kind of porter she was used to seeing, but then, nothing about this town was what she was used to. She was familiar with cities and the delicate English countryside, not this primitive-looking, dirty, little town.

Sky shook herself a little. "Yes...yes, please," she answered the man. "Are there accommodations nearby?" she asked in a drowsy voice.

"*Accomo*-what?" the man started to ask, then he quickly reached out and took hold of Sky's arm as she began to sway. "I think you need to get to the hotel, miss, unless there's someone coming for you?" He again looked at her inquisitively.

"No, no one—yes, the hotel," muttered Sky, supporting herself on the man's arm.

"I think I'll just leave them trunks there for now and get them after I get you to the hotel, miss. Come along, now." He gently guided her down the walkway. "It's not far, miss. We just cross here and up these steps."

He's really quite a gentleman, thought Sky, *even with his rough ways. Why, he's one of the nicest men I think I've ever met in America so far, except maybe for that tall stranger; now there was a man!* She dreamily walked along with the man, leaning heavily upon his arm until they reached the hotel desk.

"What have we here, Jonesy? You bring in another girl for the bride train?" The clerk behind the counter looked Sky up and down with interest.

Again Sky shook her head to wake up. "What's a bride train?" She hadn't even realized she spoke out loud until the clerk answered.

"It's leaving in two days." He clipped his words off as if giving her an advertisement. "Men from northern Minnesota need wives, so they've advertised through Colonel Stultz. He's interviewing and gathering the women together. They leave by wagon train." The clerk looked her up and down again in a rather bold way. "They'd take you, ma'am. No doubt about that."

Sky tried to clear her head. She felt fuzzy and confused. Did the man really mean that women were going to marry men they didn't know? How preposterous! But one thought stayed her. A wagon train going to Minnesota was leaving in two days.

"Do they take passengers?" she blurted.

Both men looked at her strangely. "What do you mean by *passengers?*" asked the older man, Jonesy.

"You know, passengers. I pay my fare, and they let me ride," explained Sky. *Men can be so dense*, she thought, exasperated.

The two men looked at each other then quickly looked away. "I'll be getting your trunks, miss," Jonesy said, and he ambled out of the hotel, leaving the clerk to do the explaining.

The clerk hid a smile as he said, "Do you know what a wagon train is, ma'am?"

Sky pulled herself up to her full height and looked at the man through tired and now irritated eyes. "Of course I know what a wagon train is," she replied. "It is a group of wagons, traveling together to a common destination. Will they take passengers?" She stifled a yawn.

The man gave up. "You'll have to ask Colonel Stultz that question, ma'am. Now, can I get you a room?"

Chapter 6

Sand Creek, Minnesota

Evan Trent stepped off the boardwalk and crossed the dirt street to the saloon. He was not a drinking man, his parents raised him better than that, but the saloon was where the meeting was to take place. Until the little community got a decent school or church built, it was where all the meetings took place. Sand Creek wasn't much of a town yet.

The room was crowded and noisy when he pushed open the doors. *So many? They couldn't all be here to see about getting wives!*

"Mornin,' Johnson," Evan nodded to a neighbor. *He can't be*, he thought. *I just saw his wife over at the mercantile, and there's Olson and Rueben. They're both married too. Must just be curious, like me.*

He asked for a sarsaparilla and sat down. Several others had drinks and sat visiting and laughing together.

Evan hadn't fully made up his mind yet about this mail-order bride stuff. His neighbor and friend, Michael Calloway, had ordered a bride a few months ago, and she was already on her way. He was so excited he could talk of nothing else.

Just three days ago, the two men had had a conversation about that very thing. "Just think, Evan, she'll be here soon." The two men were riding leisurely into town. Michael swept a wrinkled paper from inside his coat. "She sounds real nice too. Used to be a doctor's helper in her hometown, so she knows lots about taking care of people; she likes children and knows how to care for a home." He was reading from a letter he got in answer to his ad.

"You gotta get a wife too, Evan." He stuck the letter back in his coat pocket and appealed to his friend. "We live close enough that our wives could get real friendly, you know, help each other adjust and all."

Evan shrugged his shoulders. How could he explain how he felt to his friend? "Mike, I just don't know. I've always been taught that I need to wait on the LORD for a wife, and that when the time was right he'd bring her to me."

Michael pulled up his horse and turned to his friend while dust settled in a cloud over the two men. "I know exactly what you mean. I believe God wants the best for his children too and is interested in every part of our lives. But you know, Evan," he continued, "it's just like when we accepted Christ as our savior. We made the decision to take the gift of salvation, believing that Jesus Christ paid our way to heaven."

He rubbed his finger down his nose. "God expects us to make other decisions in our lives too. I've been praying for a wife for a long time now. I know you have too. Homesteading is lonely business when you're by yourself."

Michael swung his leg over the saddle and walked in front, leading his horse, and Evan's saddle creaked as he swung down also and joined him.

"Think of a man out in the desert praying for water. He can sit in one spot and pray all he wants, but he probably won't find water. Now if he asks for the LORD's help then starts looking, he'll probably find the water. See, God wants what's best for us, but we have to look around us too."

Evan chuckled and shook his head. He was sure his friend's illustration wouldn't hold up to any theological debates, but he got the point.

"And—" Michael stopped Evan and looked squarely in his eyes. "There aren't many women around here and none likely to be passing through. I think this advertising for a wife is God's answer to our prayers; that's why I'm doing it."

Evan rubbed his horse's neck and adjusted the bit in its mouth. He still looked uncertain. "Mike, what if she's not what you want after she gets here? What if she's not even a Christian?"

"I have faith and common sense," responded Michael immediately. "I prayed, I looked, and I believed God answered. Now I believe that God will send me the right wife. If she's not a Christian, that's a different matter. I know it's wrong to marry someone who doesn't believe in our Lord. But Evan, I'm trusting God there too. If she's not saved, she'll be saved before I marry her, or God will send me someone else. I don't want a wife so badly that I'll make a major mistake like that in my life."

Michael then laughed heartily, startling a nearby bird into flight. "As far as her looks…" He laughed again. "I only hope she won't run when she sees me!"

Evan joined in his friend's laughter. There was nothing wrong with Michael's looks. At least, nothing a little soap and water wouldn't cure.

"It's not so much what she looks like that matters to me," Michael continued in a more serious tone. "Sure, I care. Any man would. But it's what she's like on the inside. I'd like her to be cheerful and pleasant, easy to talk to yet not afraid to speak her mind. I don't want someone who just agrees with everything I say; I want a wife who tells me when I'm wrong and argues with me for the fun of it. Don't you miss someone to debate with?"

It was impossible not to catch Michael's enthusiasm. Evan nodded ruefully. "Yeah, sometimes I even start conversations with my horse and pretend he answers me." He laughed.

"See what I mean? " Michael pushed his point home. "You need a wife too. They're having a meeting in town this week to see about getting a wagon train of women to come here. I hear this Colonel Stultz has organized something like this before, so he knows what he's doing. Go to the meeting. At least hear what he has to say."

"Are you going?"

"Nah, my future wife is on her way! I've got too much to do to get ready for her, so you tell me about it later, will ya?" Michael grinned at his companion.

"Okay, Mike. You win," Evan capitulated. "I'll at least see what it's all about."

"You won't be sorry."

Evan visited with some of the men in the room, surprised at the number of men he didn't know. Homesteads had been set up all over the area, and men had come from all directions to the new town and its unusual meeting.

A heavyset man dressed in a tight banker's suit approached the front of the room. His buttons were straining to hold his shirt together over his wide girth as he held up his arms and addressed the group. "Gentlemen? Gentlemen, please, may I have your attention?"

The rumbling of voices subsided, glasses were thumped down on tables, and chairs were scraped into position as the men leaned forward to hear his words.

"My name is Colonel Stultz. I am here today to offer you fortunate men the opportunity to change your lives. Some of you are farmers, some have come from the gold-fields, and some are just beginning to homestead after your service in our recent war. Some of you men are starting to build this community: a banker, a barber, a shop owner, a blacksmith." The colonel pointed to various men in the room as he spoke, and his voice rose and became eloquent.

"You are all different, come from different backgrounds, have different likes and dislikes. But you all have one thing in common. You are bachelors. Alone. No helpmate. No one waiting for you when you come in from the fields. No one listening for your step as you enter your house."

"No one naggin' ya ta wipe yer feet!" yelled one of the married men.

Raucous laughter filled the crowded room.

"Yep, thet's right," another piped in, "and no one to be spendin' all your hard-earned money, neither."

"Hey, Johnson," called a voice from the back of the room, "I see your wife's over at Nolan's store right now spendin' all your money."

Colonel Stultz cast a worried look around the room. He tried a new tactic. "Gentlemen, I came here because I was told you were interested in obtaining wives. Now, if I've been misinformed..."

"No, you just hold on there, colonel." Nolan, the shopkeeper, stood and held up his arm. "My brother, who's over at the store right now, and I asked Colonel Stultz to come and make arrangements for wives for us and for anyone in this area who's interested. Now, he's handled affairs like this twice before, successfully," he informed the men. "So he knows what he's talking about."

Colonel Stultz rubbed a hand over his goatee. Actually, he'd only introduced his sister to her future husband and helped his friend advertise for a bride from a neighboring town. He really didn't know how to go about find-ing women willing to come north, but he was sure he could figure out something, especially if it involved making money. "The Colonel," an honorary title he'd given him-self to seem more authoritative, knew how to make money.

Nolan continued, "You married men don't belong at this meeting anyway. You already got wives. I say you leave and let us get on with it; how about it, fellas?"

The others joined in, and soon the room was cleared of the hecklers.

Colonel Stultz once again held up his arms for atten-tion then spoke. "There's something else you gentlemen must know, and you might as well know it now, since the subject of money has come up. Each of you who agrees to partake in this venture will be required to pay your bride's way here from the east, which will be by wagon train since the railroad hasn't ventured this far to the north yet, plus a small business fee to cover any additional expenses. I believe you will find the total to be quite reasonable."

He passed around some papers to the men, and com-ments filled the room.

"Ya sure it'll take that much?"

"Whew! I'll have to sell my new calf."

"That's not bad, considering we get a wife out of the deal," said Bert Davies, the banker.

Three of the men took one look at the paper then reluctantly got up and left the saloon.

Evan's eyebrows rose at the amount, but he knew he could afford it. He, too, had done some gold mining before he settled in Sand Creek, and while he hadn't struck it rich, he'd done well enough to suit himself. He was more interested in the land than in money anyway, but he had enough sense to know that he'd need money to get a good start. He finished his sarsaparilla and listened to the others.

"Mister, how do we know that once you get these women here they'll stay? What's to keep them from runnin' off soon as they get a look at us?"

The man who spoke wore a shaggy beard and was dressed in faded overalls. Evan took a closer look at the others in the room and realized that they all looked like they had just walked in from a day in the fields. *What's wrong with looking like hardworking men?* he thought. That's what they were.

"And what about them?" posed another. "What if we don't like the women you bring us? What if they're homely or old or—"

Others joined in with nods and words of agreement.

"Gentlemen, gentlemen." The colonel stretched out his arms, nearly bursting the strained buttons. "If you would let me continue, please. I can explain all these minor details."

The grumbling quieted. The men once again shifted their attention to the plump man.

"Your questions are quite reasonable, and I can answer them both. First, I have arranged with a lawyer, a personal friend of mine, to write up a document, a contract, if you will, that each of you will sign. This contract states that you promise to marry the woman who comes for you." He again raised his arms as voices rose filled with protests and questions.

"The women I interview will also sign a similar contract, pledging to marry you." The colonel had thought this through carefully, weighing all the angles. He certainly didn't want to bring a load of women out here and then get stuck with them if they refused to stay!

"This is how we guarantee that you get the wife you want and she gets the husband she wants." The colonel held up another paper. "Each of you gentlemen will fill out this paper describing what you want in a wife. You can put down physical appearance: height, weight, color of hair and eyes, whatever you want. Maybe you want her to be a certain age, or you can ask for someone who can cook, someone who can read, someone who can sing; again, whatever you want. The women will also fill out what they are looking for in a husband."

The colonel wiped his brow and continued, warming to his subject. "Then I will compare the papers and do my best to match each of you to the perfect partner. Now, you've got to realize that I can't find perfect matches for all of you, but like I said, I'll do the best I can. And with the signed contract, you will be guaranteed a wife."

The men looked around at one another, nodding their heads. Some still seemed unsure.

"Keep in mind, gentlemen," the colonel continued, "these women *want* husbands and homes just as much as you want wives. Otherwise, they'd never agree to travel way out here."

The group was won over.

"I want a pretty blonde one who can cook," spoke up the man at Evan's elbow.

"Make mine a tall one with dark hair who can read to me in the evenings," called out another.

"I want one who likes children," said Riggs, the one in overalls. "I need strong boys to help me farm."

The colonel beamed and motioned for the men to take the papers and fill them in.

Evan sat and watched. Did he want to do this? *Lord, is this the answer to my prayers?* He thought of his lonely homestead, he thought of Michael's eagerness, he thought of all the men around him who would have wives. The thought that he wouldn't if he didn't sign that contract made up his mind.

A button finally popped off the colonel's shirt as he bustled about the room, handing out the papers.

Evan stared at the paper. What did he want in a wife? He had thought about that a lot. He'd dreamed of the woman he'd make his own, but how did he write on paper all the thoughts he held in his heart? Did he write: pretty, kind, full of laughter, stuff like that? No, there was only one thing that really mattered the most to him. He wrote, "I would like my wife to be a woman who loves the LORD." He silently prayed, *Lord, it's in your hands.*

Colonel Stultz appeared very pleased. He gave Nolan the job of lining up the men to sign the contracts and to accept payment from those who had brought the money with them. Others would return with theirs. Everything was going well.

But then Ned Bolter headed for the front of the room. Ned was new to the men of Sand Creek, having arrived only a month earlier; yet he was a strong advocate for a mail-order bride. That was why his next words surprised them. "Wait a minute, fellas," he demanded their attention. "I'm not paying this man anything. What if he takes off with our money and never shows up with any women at all? No sirree. I'm not taking chances with this much money."

"But Ned, he needs the money to pay for traveling expenses to get our womenfolk here," Nolan protested.

Evan surprised himself by speaking up. "How about if we pay half now and half on delivery?" The others murmured their approval.

"*Half?*" exclaimed the colonel. "Gentlemen, I can not provide a comfortable journey for your brides on only half that amount. Do you want them to think you can't afford to pay their way, that you can't afford to take care of them? Make it two-thirds," he bargained.

"All right, mister, two-thirds now and one-third when they arrive." Bolter stepped up to the round man, towering over him. "But let me tell you something. If you don't show up with our brides, I'll hunt you down and string you up. You got that?" He pointed a dirty finger in the colonel's face.

Colonel Stultz swallowed carefully but stood his ground. "I give you my word, sir, as well as to all you gentlemen. You shall have your brides."

"See that we do," said Bolter, then he stepped back into line.

"Now gentlemen, just one more thing." The colonel was quickly back to his confident self. "I have acquired the services of a photographer." He pointed to a bored-looking man sitting in the corner of the room. "He has agreed for a very reasonable fee, a group rate shall we say, to make a photo of each of you that I may show to your prospective brides." Actually, the colonel had arranged to receive a small commission on each photo.

"Now, I know you gentlemen aren't prepared for such a thing, but not to worry." He raised his voice to speak over the complaints that had arisen. "For those of you who feel in the need of a haircut or shave first, the barber here"— he pointed to a smiling man with finely parted hair—"has agreed, also for a special price, to service your needs." The colonel smiled and stroked his goatee, making Evan wonder if the colonel wasn't padding his own pocket a bit.

"Why do you need our pictures?" asked Clyde Moore, the blacksmith. "We don't get pictures of them, do we?"

"No, of course not." The colonel smiled. "Even if I got pictures of the ladies, they wouldn't arrive before they did. But think how *your* picture will give them something to look forward to on their long journey. After all, you are all fine-looking men," he added.

There were murmurings as the men muttered to each other in complaint over this latest development. No one made a move to accommodate the colonel's request.

"Here. Form lines," the colonel directed. "I know you're not in your Sunday best, but see, the photographer here has a shirt front, collar, and tie that goes right over your own clothes and makes you look all dressed up for the occasion."

Some of the men lined up for the barber, who got right to work. Others stepped over to the photographer.

Most were embarrassed and shuffled their feet, looking at the floor. Spencer, a busy farmer from south of the town, murmured something about crops waiting.

Evan was just as embarrassed as the rest. It was one thing to just sign a contract to get married, but all this nonsense was making him want to change his mind already. Being clean shaven, he stepped over to the photographer.

Colonel Stultz was delighted. He didn't even know if he'd show the women the pictures, but he was making a tidy sum with this little maneuver.

Evan sat down for the photographer. The collar was a bit tight, and he felt his face grow hot while the other men looked on. The photographer said, "Steady...steady, hold perfectly still now."

The camera flashed, and Evan jerked. He was more nervous about the whole thing than he realized.

The photographer scowled. He knew it wouldn't be a good picture. He shrugged. He was only being paid for one; one was all he was going to take.

A tall, handsome man stepped up next. "I don't need no collar or fancy tie," Taylor Gray drawled. "My bride can take me just the way I am." He smiled at the photographer, and the camera flashed.

It was clear to Evan that the colonel was pleased with Taylor's good looks. Pleased and *calculating*, it seemed. He watched the colonel closely as the next man stepped forward.

This one had long, straggly hair and a beard to match. He was lean and hard looking.

"My bride can take me just the way I am too. Not changin' for no woman," the man muttered. He scowled at the startled photographer and snapped, "Well, go ahead and git this over with! I got work to do."

Duke Tunelle! thought Evan. *What's he doing here?* The man was practically a hermit and so mean that no one wanted him around. He looked quickly back at the colonel for his reaction and wasn't surprised at the scowl he saw cross the man's features. *Bet he's worried about not being able to find a bride for him and losing out on some money because of it. Wonder if he'll even show the women these pictures.*

"Pity the woman who gets him," muttered Bert Davies behind Evan, indicating Duke. "Ever since he lost his wife and children in that Indian raid a year ago, he's been like that. He lives alone, talks to no one. Used to be a fine man." He shook his head sadly.

The men moved through the lines quickly. The fresh haircuts stuck out like sore thumbs and the poor, rushed barber cut a few unfortunate men in his haste to shave them, but the whole process was finally over.

Timidly, the barber stepped before the photographer. "Uh, colonel, do you have room for one more on your list? I think I would like a wife too."

"Why, sure we do." The colonel beamed. He was making money today. "Step right over here."

The cantankerous photographer, who had already started to pack up his equipment, gave the barber a dirty look.

"Hurry up, will ya, bub? I'm starvin.'"

The barber pulled out his comb and slicked back his already neatly combed hair. He twisted the ends of his mustache and assumed a pose. The camera flashed.

Well, that's it, thought Evan. *Twelve of us men in need of wives. Now all the colonel has to do is find the women. Lord, help him.*

Chapter 7

New York

The expensive black carriage rolled to a stop in front of the unimpressive house. The weathered wood siding and overgrown bushes indicated a lack of upkeep either due to the absence of a man around the place or the absence of money. Hadley noted this as he exited his conveyance and made a few minor adjustments to his coat before stepping up to the door. A gray-haired woman answered the knock with a querulous, "What?"

Rudolph Hadley could see a trace of resemblance to Sky Hoffman in the woman's face, although the woman was haughty and suspicious.

"Good day, madam. May I have a word with you?"

Elaine Doane kept one hand firmly on the door and the other on the shotgun hiding inside the doorway. Her eyes traveled up and down the stranger, and a glint appeared in them when she noticed the expensive suit and gold watch.

Hadley caught the glint and knew how best to handle this woman.

"Just a few moments is all, madam. I seek information regarding a relative of yours."

The woman scowled. "Which relative? My brother or my sister or one of my late husband's?"

"I'm referring to the offspring of your sister, madam."

The scowl deepened. "You from up north?"

Hadley was perplexed but hid it well as he replied, "No, madam, of course not. I am from England, and I seek information regarding your niece, Miss Sky Hoffman."

He watched closely as Elaine's mouth dropped open. "Sky is here? Are Lucille and the baron here too?" She opened the squeaky door and looked past Hadley toward the carriage. His eyebrows shot up when he spied the gun.

"No, madam. Uh, Mrs. Doane, perhaps you should sit down. Your sister and her husband both died within the past year."

Hadley watched the woman's face whiten then return to normal. She sat on the rocker on her porch and looked at him blankly. He caught the gun as it slid from her grasp.

"Miss Hoffman recently came to the United States, and I need to find her. There is the matter of the will..." Hadley let the sentence dangle and saw the woman's eyes brighten.

"Yes. The money would all go to her, wouldn't it?"

"She's been well provided for, but I need to contact her. Can you give me any idea where she may have gone once she came here?"

"She must have told her," she muttered.

Hadley watched the woman closely, not sure what she meant.

Elaine looked at Hadley sharply. "It will cost you. I deserve some reward for sending Lucille to the baron in the first place. If you really want to know where the child is, you'll have to pay for it."

Hadley motioned to Smythe and turned again to Elaine. Now he was getting somewhere.

Chapter 8

Leaf River

Sky looked at the commotion before her then hesitantly stepped forward. She joined three other women who appeared to be waiting to speak to a portly man in a rather tight suit. Sky's quick eyes noted a button missing from his shirt.

Around them were several wagons covered with what appeared to be white sheets over large hoops. Sky had never seen anything like them before. She counted seven that she could see from where she was standing. Men were loading them with supplies, and another man was feeding some livestock—oxen, she thought.

There was something peculiar about the man who was attending to the animals. Sky watched him curiously for a few moments then suppressed a smile as he tripped over a rock, spilling the two buckets of water he was carrying and then landed on his backside, startling the oxen, that bellowed in alarm. Sky giggled softly and was surprised at the sound. How long had it been since she felt light hearted? Perhaps it was a sign that things were about to improve. She was glad now that she had put aside wearing her black mourning clothes. The decision had been difficult because she meant no disrespect to her mother, but in her attempt to escape notice from Rudolph Hadley she thought it best to be as inconspicuous as possible.

In front of her was a young woman, no, a girl, really. She held herself stiffly and looked uncomfortable. *No wonder*, thought Sky. *That dress is awful.* The girl was wearing a frilly party dress, totally unsuited to her and totally out of place in this grassy field with the bright morning sunshine beaming down.

The girl was next to approach the man.

"Good morning, miss. My name is Colonel Stultz." The colonel politely held out his hand while looking carefully at the girl, one eyebrow raised quizzically when he saw her attire. "Have you come to join our train to Sand Creek?"

"Uh, I reckon. I mean, yes, sir." The red-faced girl stumbled over her words.

"What is your name, please?"

"Uh, Ra—, I mean, Miranda. Miranda Porter, sir."

"Ah yes." The colonel consulted a paper before him. "Miranda Porter from Tennessee. I trust you had a good trip here by rail?" The girl nodded, tipping her hat askew. Embarrassed, she attempted to right it by pushing it back in place. Her precariously pinned hair toppled, and the fancy hat fell to the ground.

Sky reached down for the hat just as Miranda swung around in an attempt to catch it. She bumped Sky to one side, but before Sky could fall, Miranda reached out and caught her.

"My, that was close!" Sky laughed. "You certainly are quick." *And strong*, she thought as she adjusted her own hat. For a young woman, Miranda had amazing strength.

"Here, let me help." Sky gathered the pins she could find and quickly looped Miranda's brown hair and twisted it into a neat coil. She fastened it securely, and, where Miranda would certainly have destroyed it all by smashing the hat back on, Sky carefully took a pin from her own hair and fastened the hat securely at a becoming angle on Miranda's head. "That's much better. You're very pretty, Miss Porter."

Miranda's red face deepened in color, but she thanked Sky with her eyes.

Colonel Stultz had watched the whole procedure with amusement and interest. The young Miss Porter was extremely clumsy, but she would be acceptable to most of the men on his list. The beauty behind her would be an easy match. He spoke to the ladies.

"Miss Porter, if you would look over these papers, please. You can read, can't you?"

"My granddad taught me." Miranda spoke softly.

"Good, good. Then you just go right over there with the others and look these over. Now, miss..." The colonel directed his attention to Sky. "Will you also be joining our train to Sand Creek?"

Sky stepped forward and smiled at the man, aware of his appraising look. Her dark green dress with the rows of buttons down the bodice, tucked in waist, and slight bustle had a definite English flavor and made her stand out from the other women who, apart from Miranda Porter, were serviceably dressed in skirts and shirtwaists. A dark green hat, perched attractively on her golden hair—which was wrapped in a simple, elegant knot behind her head—set off the blue in her eyes.

Sky's mother had been the only person except for a few friends at boarding schools who had ever called her beautiful. Sky was mature enough to know her mother doted on her, perhaps more than most mothers would in an effort to make up for the baron's lack of interest.

She spoke, "I would like very much to travel with the train, sir, but only as a passenger, not as one of the brides. I have business I need to attend to, but I have no interest in getting married at this time."

"A passenger?" Both eyebrows rose. "This is not a wagon train for passengers, miss. Haven't you read our ad? The men from the area of Sand Creek desire wives and are willing to pay their passage."

"I, too, am willing to pay my passage," said Sky.

Colonel Stultz's interest was piqued. Here was a way to earn a little extra money. The problem was that he needed two more women contracted as brides. The train was leaving the next day, and he dare not arrive without a bride for each man.

The colonel had not gone all the way east for the women. In an effort not to spend too much of the money, thereby assuring more for himself, he had sent ads to be put in the newspapers of several eastern towns. The ads requested that interested women meet here in Leaf River, the end of the railroad line. The women provided their own transportation this far. Quite a clever move, he thought. But he still needed two more women, and he had begun to worry. Perhaps he could persuade this one.

"I'm sorry, Miss—?"

"Hoffman, sir, and I believe you said your name was Colonel Stultz?"

"That's right, Miss Hoffman. I truly am sorry, but we can only accommodate women on this trip who have signed contracts with us to become the wives of the men from Sand Creek. I assure you, Miss Hoffman, it is the only safe way to venture north. A woman who is not spoken for should never travel where there are men who are desperate for wives; they would even resort to kidnapping." He, of course, exaggerated; the men were very respectful of women, but he hoped to convince her.

"What kind of contract do these women sign?" Sky questioned curiously, ignoring the man's obvious blathering.

"They sign a paper pledging to marry the man they are matched up with once we arrive. The men have signed similar contracts."

"Why would anyone agree to marry someone they had never met and even sign a paper so that there's no way to back out?" Sky was incredulous.

The colonel looked at Sky and at her expensive clothing and said, "Miss Hoffman, obviously you have never been poor and without hope of a future."

Her mother's face flashed before her.

"Many of these women have sold all that they have to get here. They've left behind all that is familiar to them because they want a life of their own, which includes having their own husband and children and home. For the men it's a little different. They have land or a mine or cattle or some reason why they can't leave to find a wife. They are lonely and desire a family as well. Do you begrudge either the method they've chosen?"

Sky shook her head and slowly started away. There must be another way north to find her twin. She'd find it, but she would not sign herself over to a man just to get there.

"If you change your mind, we're leaving in the morning," the colonel called after her. He hated to lose her.

There wasn't much to the small town. Sky stopped and asked everywhere about travel to Minnesota. The only solutions offered her were to either buy a horse and ride alone, which was out of the question, or take the railroad back until she found a different line that could take her further north. Unfortunately, she didn't have enough money to travel the railroad trains that long.

She stopped on the boardwalk and sighed deeply.

An old woman was struggling up the steps with a heavy basket of eggs on her arm. Sky stepped forward and placed an arm under the woman and took hold of the basket.

"Here, let me help you with that," she said. The woman gratefully leaned on Sky for support as they reached the top step.

Without warning, Sky felt a tug at her arm and saw a flash of blue. She turned and saw the heels and back of a young boy disappear behind the building.

"My bag!" cried Sky. Steadying the old woman took several seconds, but finally Sky was free to pursue the lad. She raced around the corner and then around the next, but he was gone.

Seeing Jonesy across the street at the train depot, Sky headed his way, keeping her eyes open for the boy.

"Mr. J, Jonesy! Wh, where might I...find the constable in...this town!" Sky was out of breath from her chase. She needed that bag; it contained all the money she had left!

"*Consta*–What?" Jonesy took off his cap and scratched his head.

"Who enforces...the law in this town?" Sky spoke slowly, enunciating each word. "My bag was just stolen by a little ruffian."

"A *what—ian*?" Jonesy backed away from the look in Sky's eyes. "We got no lawman right now, miss. One travels through here ever once in a while, but he ain't due for weeks."

Sky groaned in exasperation. "Now what am I going to do?" She walked into the small train station and dropped down on the bench. At least her mother's letter was still safe back at the hotel; for that Sky was thankful, though what she would do if her bag wasn't retrieved she had no idea.

Jonesy stood in the doorway, wanting to help but not knowing how. "Maybe you could describe this—*muff-ian* to me. I might know who—"

He broke off his sentence and turned to look over his shoulder. A rider was coming.

A big, gray horse stopped outside the building, and Sky glanced through the window at the man riding it. He was an older man, average build, his clothes dusty from the trail. Sky looked away, uninterested, and pondered what she was going to do next.

"You got a saloon in this town?" the man asked Jonesy. "Sure need to wet my whistle."

"Building on the left's the saloon; off to the right there's a well with the coldest, clearest water this side of the Mississippi." Jonesy pointed. "Great for wetting whistles."

The man snorted.

"Right. Listen, train-man, I'm looking for someone. Lookin' for a young lady who might've come here by train in the last few days. Name's..." He hunted in his pocket for a scrap of paper and read, "Hoffman. Sky Hoffman. Ya ever heard of her?"

"Nope, can't say as I've ever heard that name before." Jonesy again took off his cap and scratched his head. "Purty name, though, ain't it?"

Sky's head jerked up and her heart started pounding. *Who is that man? Why is he looking for me?* She was surprised Jonesy hadn't told the man she was right inside; then she realized Jonesy didn't know her name.

"This gal I'm lookin' for *is* real purty. She's got real long, blonde hair and eyes that are blue. She's about this high off the ground"—he motioned with his hand—"and real trim, if you know what I mean. Wears real fancy dresses too."

Sky crouched on the bench, making herself as small as possible. Her mouth was dry. Jonesy surely knew who the man was describing now. There just weren't that many people in this town not to. She strained to hear his answer.

"Well now, mister, she sounds real nice. Most of the women we see around here have dark hair. Mind you, I've seen some blue-eyed blondes in my day. Prefer the dark ones myself."

"So you haven't seen this Sky Hoffman? She didn't get off the train here?" the man persisted.

"Like I said, I don't know anyone by that name, and I handle all the train's comings and goings." Jonesy's look was apologetic. "Sorry, mister. If you hold on a minute there, I'll fetch ya some of that water. Best yet."

The stranger grumbled but waited as Jonesy returned with the water. "Reckon I better be getting on my way, then." He looked longingly over at the saloon after he had drunk from the dipper, but he didn't dismount. "I gotta backtrack this train and check the other stops. If you do meet up with this gal, send for me, will ya? Name's Conners. There's a gent in New York mighty anxious to get her back."

He dug his heels into the horse's sides and rode off. Dust settled back into place, and Jonesy turned back to Sky.

"Like I was sayin,' miss. If you can describe this thief?"

Sky just stared at him. "You didn't tell him I was here. You lied for me."

"Hold on a minute there, miss. If you recall, I never told the man a lie at all, except maybe about preferring dark-haired gals." He cast a grin her way.

Jonesy looked for the thief and asked all around town to no avail. Her money was gone. Hadley's detectives were looking for her. Even if she could find a job in this town, she couldn't stay. He'd find her.

She had to take that wagon train.

Leaf River

Before the evening became dark, Sky again approached Colonel Stultz. He smiled. Her bag lay hidden in his wagon where he'd placed it after paying off the boy. He had expected her sooner.

Another woman stepped up to the colonel at the same time, so Sky motioned for her to go ahead. The woman held a small baby in her arms, and a little boy about two years old clung to her skirts.

She pleaded, "Colonel, I know you told me once before that you wouldn't take me because of my children. I'm begging you. I have no way to care for them or myself since my husband died. Please take us with you."

The colonel heaved a sigh. He did need another bride for the train, but he didn't want one with children. The men never agreed to that, contract or not, and he didn't want to be stuck with her. "Please understand, Mrs. Scott, I would be delighted to take you, but my wagon master, Mr. Dewell, is against it. He's taken trains before, and he says they're too hard on youngsters. I'm sorry." Using the wagon master as an excuse was the quickest thing that came to the colonel's mind.

Tears filled the woman's eyes. "You've never known what it's like to be without hope." She turned away.

Sky stopped her. "Wait." Was this how her mother had felt when she agreed to marry the baron? No hope? Sky had never been in a position where she had no hope. Even now, when she felt forced to take the wagon train, she didn't feel that way. There were probably other solutions if she looked. But she needed to get out of this town in a hurry, and she needed to get to Minnesota to find her twin. She'd deal with the man waiting at the end when she got there. But she was not completely without hope like this woman.

Sky looked at Colonel Stultz while the woman waited, watching her. "Sir, do you still want me on your wagon train?"

The colonel was delighted but wary. "Yes, Miss Hoffman. That is, if you agree to come as a bride."

"I wish to come," Sky replied. "But only if you take Mrs. Scott and her children as well."

The colonel hid a smile. That would take care of the last two women he needed. He'd take a chance on the children too, if necessary.

"You win, Miss Hoffman. Mrs. Scott, I will make one request of you. Keep those children hidden from Dewell

for the first couple of days, or you may be sent back."
Hopefully his quick lie wouldn't get noticed, but once it
was begun he had to follow through with it. The woman
quickly nodded.

"Now, ladies, please fill out these papers. In approxi-
mately two months you will become the wives of two very
lucky men."

Chapter 9

Iowa

Russ Newly had been in the saddle for weeks. He was tired, and his horse was tired, but now he was almost to the town.

It was time to check in with his boss. Fortunately, things had gone well on his last job, and he could give a good report. His boss would be pleased.

The saddle creaked as Russ stepped down in front of the hotel. He couldn't remember the last time he'd slept in a bed. He rubbed his face. He needed a shave, probably a haircut, and most definitely a bath. All in good time, he thought, but business first; always business first.

He was still far enough to the south that there was a telegraph line set up. Telegraph poles were beginning to dot the countryside, but they weren't in every town yet and not to the north of this one. He headed for the telegraph office.

The middle-aged man behind the desk looked up as Russ entered. He was just finishing his lunch. A plate was pushed to one side with chicken bones piled high on it, and a napkin still stuck out of his collar as he busily licked his fingers.

"Afternoon. What can I do for you today?"

The leftover aroma of the food made Russ's stomach ache with hunger. "That food come from the hotel, or does your wife bring you lunch?"

"It's from the hotel. They serve the best chicken in town if you're looking for a meal, mister." The man stood up and walked over to the counter Russ was leaning on. He remembered the napkin and pulled it out to wipe off his sticky fingers. "I got no wife. The land is too rugged yet for most women. I hear, though, that you can place an ad for a wife in an eastern newspaper and if you pay her way, some woman will travel out here and marry you. Ever hear of such a thing?"

Russ laughed. "Sounds like a good way to lose some money."

"No, I'm serious, mister. I know of at least two men who got wives that way. Been thinking of doing it myself."

Russ tipped his Stetson back on his head. "Advertise for a wife, hey?" A picture of a young woman with long golden hair and skirts flying flashed through his mind. "No, that's not for me. I prefer to see who I'm going to marry before I agree to marry her." *What nonsense*, he thought. *No man in his right mind would do a thing like that.*

"I need to send a telegram to Chicago."

The man scurried about and found paper and pencil for him. As Russ scribbled his message, he asked, "Have you got anything for me? Name's Rex Newton." He never used his own name on jobs like this.

"Let me see. Yes, Mr. Newton. Looks like you got two messages. They came about a week ago. Sometimes I get telegrams that sit in that cubbyhole for months and then one day someone like you rides into town and asks for it. Seems slower to me than the Pony Express used to be, and we all thought that was fast."

He's a talker, thought Russ. Then he said, "Let me see that telegram again. I forgot something." He added a few more words, laid down money for the telegram, and picked up his messages. "Think I'll head to the hotel for some of that chicken. Smells really good. Thanks a lot."

Russ walked outside again and adjusted his hat over his eyes. There was a bench alongside the building and no one around, so he moved to it and sat down.

The first message was from his boss. He already had another job lined up for him, but this time he'd be working with a close friend of his. It would be good to see Hank again; it sure beat working alone.

The second was from Hank, telling him where to meet him and when. The only other information he got was that he was to meet up with a wagon train.

The bench felt good. He stretched out his legs and let his head fall back to rest against the building. The warm sun made him drowsy, and though he knew he had to get moving, he allowed himself a few minutes of rest. Only a moment, and there she was in his mind again.

Miss Hoffman.

He wished he knew her first name. Mentally he replayed the scene with her and the English gent.

Did she manage to get away from him, Lord? Is she safe now? Why am I thinking of her all the time? I only saw her for a few minutes. He shook his head in an effort to clear his mind for the job before him, but somehow he knew getting the lovely Miss Hoffman off his mind was not going to be easy.

Russ stood and stretched his tired muscles. He better skip lunch. He'd have to take care of his horse first then get a shave, haircut, and bath before supper. He'd at least get one night's sleep in a bed; then he had a lot of riding to do in the next week or so.

Chapter 10

Wagon Train

Traveling by wagon train has to be the slowest, dirtiest, most painful way of travel there is, thought Sky. She laughed to herself when she remembered requesting to ride as a passenger on the wagon train. *No one rides this train!*

She walked beside her wagon while Miranda drove the oxen. Sky could ride horseback, and she could handle a small buggy pulled by a single horse, but she wasn't sure what to do with two oxen. She'd learn, though. She wasn't going to leave it all for Miranda. Sky knew how sore a person could get just riding on the wagon. She groaned and rubbed her backside. No, she'd learn and give Miranda her turn to walk.

They were barely into their third day on the trail. When Sky had arrived at the wagons the morning they left, the colonel was pairing off the women who would ride together. Miranda caught sight of Sky and walked over to her. Shyly she asked, "Miss Hoffman, uh, would you—could we ride together?"

"I'd love to Miranda, but call me Sky. We'll make a good team, won't we?" Sky was full of enthusiasm that first day; after all, she was on her way to finding her twin sister.

Twelve women paired off into six of the wagons. The seventh wagon was for Colonel Stultz and also for the extra food supplies, though each wagon carried a portion of the food as well so that none was overcrowded.

Two problems arose right at the beginning. One was that Violet Boothe, a pretty but haughty girl, refused to share a wagon with Martha Scott and her two children.

"I won't be crowded out by a thumb-sucking brat and a crying baby," she protested.

Gertie Curran took Violet's arm. "Share with me, Violet. We'll have lots of fun together."

The two walked away whispering together and casting glances back at Martha.

Sky saw that Martha looked worried. It was bad enough trying to keep the presence of two children a secret from the wagon master, and Violet wasn't helping. Sky started for Martha then stopped when she noticed a small, blonde woman step up and gently place a hand on Martha's arm.

"Hi. I'm Angelina Sharp. Would it be all right if we shared?"

The young woman seems sweet, thought Sky. *She's just what Martha needs.* She saw Angelina reach for the baby and knew things would work out.

The other problem was Sky's luggage. No other woman had brought as much along as Sky had. Even Martha, who lived right in the town, left most of her belongings or sold what she could in the short time she had. These American women knew what wagon train travel was like. But Sky wouldn't give up her trunks.

"It's enough that I'm coming along in the first place, Colonel Stultz," she protested when he asked her to leave one behind. "I'm not giving them up."

Miranda tried to help her. "It's okay," she said. "We can put both trunks in our wagon. I'll sleep outside underneath the wagon. I like sleeping outside."

"No, Miranda, that wouldn't be fair," Sky said. "Colonel Stultz has extra space in his wagon. I'm sure he won't mind, will you, colonel?" Sky smiled at the man as she held his gaze.

"Oh all right, but if we have to lighten our load later on, your trunk will be the first thing to go." The defeated man stomped away.

The first two nights on the trail, Sky had gone to bed exhausted. She couldn't even keep her eyes open while eating their evening meal.

Tonight I'll do better, she thought. *Why, I haven't even gotten to know any of the women yet. Miranda never seems to get tired.* Sky looked up at her.

Miranda smiled from the wagon seat. "Are your legs feeling better today, Sky?" she called.

"I guess so," Sky answered. She walked closer so she wouldn't need to yell. Her aches and pains seemed to amuse Miranda. "Who's turn is it to cook today?"

"The O'Donnells'. We're tomorrow."

The O'Donnells, Gretchen and Bridget, were sisters who shared a wagon. The women had agreed to take turns doing the chores, so each day a different pair would do the fire-building and cooking, another would do the cleaning up, and the rest would haul water and gather more wood for the next fire. They all took care of their own clothes washing.

Sky glanced at Miranda again. Today Miranda had on a different dress, but this one was another frilly affair. She was puzzled. Doesn't the girl know what to wear? Even Sky, with all her fancy clothes, had sensible skirts. She even had two riding habits along, though one was quite elaborate. She didn't understand Miranda's choice of clothing, but it was none of her business.

Supper tasted so good that evening that Sky felt embarrassed at the amount she had eaten. *Must be the fresh air,* she thought. That and the walking every day were only the beginning, she found. Settling the wagon train into a circle each night, unhooking the oxen and leading them to water, besides all the other chores, seemed to use up all her energy. Sky realized that she had never worked so hard in her whole young life as she had the last few days. Surprisingly, she also realized that despite her inward sorrow she had never been happier.

It was a perfect evening. The supper fire crackled pleasantly while the clean up was done. Many of the women sat around talking, and for the first time Sky took a good look at them.

The O'Donnells were almost look-alikes. Both had reddish hair from their Irish ancestry and a sprinkling of freckles, and they were about the same height. But the resemblance ended with their looks. Gretchen, the older one, was quiet but pleasant. Bridget, only a year younger, was bubbly and outgoing. She had talked all through supper.

"Don't ya just be a wondering what our husbands-to-be look like? I want me a tall one with dark hair and eyes and who smiles and laughs a lot. Ah! That would be heaven on earth to live with such a man!"

"It would be heaven on earth for sure if you'd let these poor starving women eat in peace," her sister teased.

Sky smiled with the others; she liked the O'Donnells. Their story was simple but sad. The two sisters had been sent to America by their family in Ireland in the hopes that they would find better lives for themselves. The family farm was overcrowded and money scarce. The girls had arrived in New York only to find the relatives they had been sent to lived under similar circumstances except they were in a crowded, filthy city instead of on a farm.

Since the Irish weren't welcome in the east, the only work for them was in a textile factory where they were given the lowliest of jobs at the lowest wages. The girls were hard workers and could have endured the long hours, heavy labor, and dangerous working conditions, but the constant persecution over being Irish immigrants eventually led them to answer the ad with the blessing of relatives who could only be eased by having the burden of extra mouths to feed lifted.

Gretchen and Bridget hoped to find a chance for happiness by traveling farther west, and they dreamed of husbands and families close by each other. Their optimism despite their hardships was another thing that Sky admired about them.

Sky wished she could say that she liked Violet and Gertie. She glanced over at the pair sitting by their wagon. Gertie wasn't so bad, really. Sky had listened to her story earlier. Gertie was raised by an overbearing aunt who cast her more in the role of a servant than a relative. She never had any friends her own age, which seemed to explain her devotion now to Violet. When Gertie's aunt passed away, she had to leave their rented house with only a small inheritance to live on. She answered the ad because she did not know what else she could do. *So little self-worth,* thought Sky. She hoped Gertie found a husband who would treasure her.

It was soon evident to all that Violet expected a free ride. She got headaches, she explained, so she couldn't stoop to pick up firewood or carry buckets of water. It was better that Gertie drove the team so that she, Violet, could lie down in the back and rest.

That was bad enough, thought Sky, but Gertie idolized her new friend. It sickened Sky to see her carry Violet's bucket and wait on her at mealtimes. Gertie was a timid follower, and it surprised Sky that Gertie had found the courage to become a mail-order bride. The reason Violet was along was unclear, unless she couldn't find anyone willing to marry her wherever she was from.

Sky's perusal was interrupted when Janet Conly stood and addressed the group.

"Ladies, I think it would be a good idea if we ended each evening with Bible reading and prayer," she announced. Janet was a tall, authoritative woman, and it only seemed natural that she take a leadership role. *Reminds me of a governess I once had*, thought Sky. Janet's traveling companion was Nola Anderson, a quiet, worried woman. Miranda told Sky that Nola was another widow on the train.

Janet looked over the seated ladies. "Please, go get your Bibles from your wagons and bring them with you each evening from now on."

Gracious! thought Sky as the women scurried off. *They act like she's the local school mistress. She does have that air*, she decided, looking at her.

Janet waited, tapping her foot until the others returned. Sky had remained seated, and Janet eyed her questioningly.

"I don't own a Bible, Miss Conly." Sky wasn't prepared for the shock on Janet's face. Clearly she was an exception, for all the others returned carrying Bibles in their hands.

Miranda sat down by Sky, noticing her empty hands. "I'll share with you," she said. She opened the large, worn book. "This was my granddad's. We read together all the time." Miranda's voice was sad.

"Is your grandfather still alive?" Sky asked gently.

Tears welled up in Miranda's eyes. She blinked rapidly. "No, he died a month ago. That's why I'm here. I promised him—"

Miranda's words were interrupted as Janet spoke again.

"We will start with Genesis. Apparently there are some here who need to start at the beginning." Her eyes again scorched Sky before looking to her Bible.

Colonel Stultz watched from behind his wagon where he couldn't be seen by the women. He wasn't going to get in on any Bible reading! Wasn't there a man on his list who wanted a religious woman? "Someone who loves the LORD," he'd put. Odd. He'd have to pair him with Janet. Poor fellow. The colonel shook his head as he walked away.

Sky enjoyed the reading despite Janet's attitude. The Bible hadn't been a part of her education or upbringing, probably because of her mother's unhappiness with God. Sky listened politely as Janet's prayer droned on and on. Then the women began retiring to their wagons.

As Sky and Miranda also prepared to leave, Hector Riley, the man whom Sky had seen trip with the water buckets, walked by leading some of the oxen. The colonel had hired him and another man to help the wagon master handle the affairs of running the wagon train. The other man's name was Crane. Sky couldn't help the shiver that ran through her when she thought of the rough-looking man. Crane seemed...dangerous. Fortunately he stayed away from all the women completely, for he rode ahead of the train as scout. Hector's job was taking care of the animals and riding the rear of the train as guard.

Sky smiled kindly at Hector as he passed. "Good evening, Mr. Riley, and how are you?" She liked Hector despite his awkwardness.

Hector stopped abruptly and stammered, "Fine e-evening, I'm...g-good...I mean, good...evening, I'm fine." He stood, looking embarrassed, pushing the toe of his boot in the dirt. He cast his eyes around in all directions to avoid looking directly at her or Miranda, who was behind her, until he noticed the brim of his hat. Remembering his manners, he grabbed it off his head.

Sky's eyes widened. Never in her life had she seen hair stick straight up in the air. The brown mass still held the shape of Hector's Stetson. She heard a soft gasp from Miranda. Sky pulled her eyes away, nodded, and moved to pass in front of Hector on her way to the wagon, but at that moment the oxen, impatient for their evening meal, pushed into Hector's back.

Looking back, the next events would later remind Sky of a time when she fell off her horse. All motions slowed down so that instead of a few seconds it seemed like several minutes were held in space.

Miranda yanked her out of the way as Hector stumbled forward, desperately trying to keep his balance. His flailing arms caught the bucket of wash water left after supper dishes and tipped it over his shoulders as he fell to the ground with a thud. A cloud of dust was followed by the dirty, soapy water that gracefully rose into the air then descended in an array of glistening droplets and suds over the sprawled out man. Miranda jumped to control the oxen.

The other women stopped and turned at the commotion as Sky ran and knelt by Hector.

"Are you all right, Mr. Riley?" Concern mixed with muffled amusement was in her voice.

He grinned at her and opened his mouth to speak when Violet broke in.

"So the village half-wit has been hired to guard for us. My, don't I feel safe!" she said sarcastically.

Sky cast her a dark look then reached down to help Hector up.

Hector goodnaturedly picked up his hat, thanked Miranda as he took the ropes from her, and walked off with the oxen.

"My goodness! That young man is a bit clumsy, isn't he?" Sky and Miranda both swung around to defend Hector, but the woman speaking was smiling genuinely and without malice. "I'm Isabelle Pry, but call me Belle. Everyone does. I thought you and Miss Porter handled that very well, Miss Hoffman."

The woman was in her early forties, a bit plump, and wore a pleasant expression. She smiled at Sky and Miranda.

"You're wondering what a woman my age is doing in a group like this, aren't you, girls? Come, join me by the fire a minute. Bertha won't mind if I come in later. She's a sweet lady; we've become good friends already. Besides, it's too nice an evening to waste."

The three women settled near the dying fire, and Sky watched the burning embers a moment before turning to Belle.

"Are you widowed?" she asked.

"Oh no, dear, I've never been married." The older woman laughed softly then sighed. "No, I *had* the chance once, but I didn't take it. I've always regretted it.

"Twenty years ago my sister married the man I loved. He wanted to marry me, but my sister came between us. To make a long story short, he chose to marry her instead. I was heartbroken and turned away all other callers. I stayed home and cared for my ailing mother; then a year ago she died, and last month I went to my sister's for a visit. It was the first time I had been in their home."

Sky liked Belle's pleasant voice. Even while she described her heartache and misery her face revealed that all was well with her. The fire sputtered, flamed, then glowed again, but Sky's and Miranda's attentions were drawn to the petite woman.

"My sister wanted me to stay on with them. At first I was grateful; then I realized she wanted me as a housemaid and not as a family guest. I would not stay and let her make my life as miserable as I could see she had made her husband's. Then I found the ad for brides to go to Sand Creek. It didn't have any age limits on it, so I asked God for guidance and left on the next stage. You should have seen my sister's face." She chuckled. "She looked almost as surprised as Colonel Stultz's did when I arrived."

Belle enjoyed her laugh, and the girls smiled with her.

"The colonel told me there were a couple of gentlemen of suitable age for me to choose from. You young girls probably think I'm crazy, but I don't care what he looks like. I just want him to have a good heart. I could love any man who had a good heart, even if he were as clumsy as that young Riley."

Miranda shifted positions, and Sky glanced at her curiously, then, looking back to Belle, said, "I'm happy for you, Belle. I hope he's everything you want. We'd better call it a night, though, or we won't be ready to roll in the morning. We'll talk again."

They said their good nights and retired to their wagons.

As Sky shifted for a better position in the crowded wagon, she heard Miranda sigh.

"Something wrong, Miranda?" she asked softly.

"Sky, what did you put on that paper? What kind of husband do you want? I didn't know what to put, so I left it blank." Miranda moaned.

"I left mine blank too," Sky admitted. "I don't even want a husband, you see. I just need to get there so I can find my twin sister, whom I've never met. We were separated at birth, and all I know is that she was taken by wagon train to Minnesota twenty years ago."

Miranda quietly digested this information before exclaiming, "A twin sister! But how will you know where to look? Minnesota is a big place. What about your husband?" she whispered.

"I'll cross those bridges when I come to them," murmured the sleepy Sky. "Good night, Miranda."

Miranda's sleepless eyes stared out at the stars long into the night.

Chapter 11

Wagon Train

Several days passed, and Sky continued to be amazed at Miranda's stamina. Day after day she drove the wagon, patiently showing Sky how to do it for herself. Night after night Sky dropped off to sleep before Miranda did. She felt guilty that she couldn't stay awake, for she now knew Miranda needed to talk to her.

It had started at the afternoon meal when she and Miranda were in charge of cooking for the day. Once again Miranda amazed Sky, for while Sky knew a little about cooking, having watched the baron's cook on occasion, she had never seen cooking done over an open fire, but Miranda handled it like she did it every day. Her meals soon were the ones everyone looked forward to, for they were never under cooked or overcooked, and they often contained interesting flavors. Sky discovered that Miranda picked many herbs and roots and leaves along the trail or near their resting sites and used them to season the food.

Sky was assisting Miranda over the stewpot when some of the lace on Miranda's frilly dress caught on fire. They both slapped at it, and Sky splashed water from the bucket on it so no one was burned or hurt. The incident would have gone unnoticed had not Violet witnessed it.

"My, aren't we graceful today!" Violet looked around and, seeing an audience, continued, walking toward the two women, "And so dressed up too! Are we having a ball? Oh, but you've been dressed for a ball since we started, haven't you? Shouldn't you save your party dresses for your husband to see?"

Miranda's face paled, and her grip tightened on the spoon she held.

"Maybe Hector will dance with you at the ball. You'd make a lovely couple, you and Hector. You're both as graceful as two oxen." Violet sneered and Gertie giggled. Sky saw Hector walking toward the stream with buckets for the oxen. His back was stiff and straight.

Sky spoke loudly so that all the others could hear, "We'll be needing more wood for our fire, Violet. Would you get it, please?"

"No, I'm afraid I can't," Violet objected in a pouty voice. She turned from Miranda to face Sky. "You will remember that I have trouble with headaches, and I find that bending for wood worsens them." She smiled sweetly at Sky, ignoring Miranda. "I'm afraid you'll have to muss one of your own dresses, Miss Hoffman, and do it yourself."

Sky bristled. "I believe your American history books make mention of a pilgrim captain by the name of John

Smith. He told the men of Jamestown that if they would not work, they could not eat."

Sky looked over at Janet Conly. "And doesn't the Bible say something like that as well, Miss Conly?" Miranda had told Sky about the verse the night before when Violet's name had come up.

"Second Thessalonians 3:10 is the verse to which you refer." Janet's head bobbed up and down. "I'm glad to see you are learning the Scriptures, Miss Hoffman." She primly folded her hands in front of her. "I believe what Miss Hoffman is saying is exactly correct, Miss Boothe. You must do your share around here. We all have aches and pains to deal with; yours are no exception."

"Time to eat," called Sky. She looked anxiously at Miranda, who slipped away as the others gathered around. "I'm sorry, Violet, but you will not be served until the wood has been brought in." Sky was surprised at her own daring, but she would not back down to the rude girl.

"You can't tell me what to do," snapped Violet, her pretty face turning ugly.

Colonel Stultz stepped near the fire. He had kept out of the women's affairs as much as possible, and he intended to continue to do so, but Violet's behavior could not be allowed any longer. The train still had a long way to go.

"Miss Boothe," he spoke directly to the girl. "You were asked if you had any health problems before our journey began. I would not have taken you if I had known, and the men who hired me will not take a crippled woman either. I'm afraid I shall have to leave you off at the next town."

"What about my contract?" demanded Violet. "That guarantees me a husband, you said."

"It does not apply if you lied," stated the colonel without blinking an eye. The two stared at each other until finally Violet backed down.

"Oh, all right! I'll get your firewood." Her eyes pierced Sky as she stomped by.

Miranda helped with supper preparations and then left again without eating. Sky found her later outside the wagon circle, sitting on a rock, looking up at the moon.

Sky thought she had approached the rock quietly, but Miranda turned before she reached her and said, "Sky, I'm sorry."

"You want to talk about it?" Sky joined her on the rock. Neither noticed the form in the shadows nearby.

Miranda took a deep breath of the night air and let it out slowly. "My folks died in an influenza epidemic when I was two."

Sky's eyebrows raised. *What does that have to do with Violet?*

Miranda noticed Sky's confused expression. "Please, Sky, you won't understand today if you don't know my past."

"Go ahead, Miranda. I want to know. I want to help."

"Well, let's start with my name, then," continued Miranda. "My granddad always called me Randi. Would you, Sky? I sure miss hearing it. No one ever called me Miranda before except maybe when I was a baby."

Sky nodded and pulled her knees up under her as she waited for Miranda to go on.

"My granddad raised me by himself in the Tennessee mountains. I shouldn't say by himself, I guess, because he had some help from the Indians. He was a mountain man. I spent more of my time outdoors than I ever did in the cabin. Sky, I know how to read and write, but I also know all there is to living in the wild. I can cook and bake on a campfire. I can hunt and trap and fish. I know all the herbs and medicines in the forest. My granddad taught me everything; everything except how to be a young lady.

"Granddad knew he was dying. About three months ago he took me into a town and told the lady in the store I needed some nice clothes. He said I needed to look like a young lady."

Miranda chuckled sadly then was silent. Sky waited, fascinated as she watched the emotions flitting over her friend's face.

"Sky, I grew up wearing buckskins and moccasins. The lady took one look at me and figured she had her work cut out for her."

She lifted the lacy fabric of her dress. "Unfortunately, she went too far in the other direction. Granddad agreed to buying four dresses like this with hats and shoes to match."

Miranda bit her lip, and her voice sounded husky as she continued. "Then Granddad and I spent the night in town at a hotel. First time I'd ever done that. The next day was Sunday, and we went to church. Granddad and I always held our own Sunday church time together, just the two of us, so I didn't know what church was like.

"People stared at Granddad in his buckskins and me in a dress 'fit for a ball.' At least I was less out of place there than on this wagon train."

Miranda swallowed and had to choke out the next words. "Granddad meant well, Sky, but he approached every young man there to see if he needed a wife. I was so embarrassed! Of course, all the men shied away from me like I was a horse with two heads. No man wants a wife forced on him."

The moonlight dimmed as light clouds passed by, and Sky was aware of the coolness of the rock beneath her.

"Granddad finally realized that wasn't going to work. A couple of months passed, and I thought we could forget about finding me a husband, but Granddad didn't want me left all alone when he died. I don't think he would have ever acted like that if he hadn't known how short his time was. It was then that he saw the ad about brides needed in Sand Creek. He grabbed onto that like a drowning man does a rope. He said it was 'an answer to prayer' and he told me to get ready and pack up because I was going to get married.

"It was the only time I ever fought with Granddad about anything. We squabbled for days. He said I was ornery and stubborn. I said I ought to be; I was just like him.

"On the day he died, he made me promise I would go through with this. Sky, I would rather stay all alone in the

Tennessee mountains and never see another person again as long as I live than marry a man I didn't even know."

Sky held out her hand to Miranda. "I know, Miranda, I mean Randi. I like your name; it suits you. I feel the same way, so what do we do? We've signed the contracts."

"Well, I know one thing I haven't done. I haven't prayed about this. I've been so sad about losing Granddad and so mad about keeping this promise that I guess I forgot about God. Granddad didn't, though. I remember that he prayed about my future husband ever since I became a teenager."

"I don't know much about God, Randi. When you talk like that it sounds different from how Janet talks, yet you're both talking about the same God. Can you—?"

"Shhh!" interrupted Randi. "Someone's out there." She pointed toward the shadows.

Sky tried looking where Randi was pointing, but the moon was now shadowed by clouds, and all the trees seemed to take on grisly human form in her mind. She shivered.

"He's gone." Randi seemed very sure, but Sky was uneasy.

"Can we...go back to the...wagon now?" Fear crept into her voice, and she was amazed at Randi's calmness.

"Sure. I'll check for tracks tomorrow. I'm sure it's nothing to worry about, but we need to be more careful." She soothed her friend.

Sky gripped Randi's arm as together they headed back to the camp.

Chapter 12

Wagon Train

The next morning the girls awoke to the wake-up call. Randi, as usual, opened her eyes instantly and sat up. Sky, not yet used to the early time, rolled over and groaned.

Randi good-naturedly shook her friend. "Come on, Sky! Wagons have to roll."

Sky rolled over and sat up. "These wagons don't roll. They bounce and creak and sway." She stretched and yawned. "Randi, have you figured out who that was in the shadows last night?"

Randi's forehead puckered. "Whoever it was, he was very good. I know most sounds of the night and can usually hear when there's a person around. I don't want to alarm you, Sky, but it may have been an Indian. They are the quietest people I know in the wilderness. As quiet and careful as I've learned to be, I'm still not quite as good as they are. I'll check for tracks before we break camp."

Sky's face showed concern as she reached for her dress. Randi opened her small trunk and began to pull out the dress folded on top. Her face looked miserable, and Sky couldn't bear to see it, yet she was hesitant, afraid to hurt Randi's feelings.

"Randi, would you like to try one of my skirts today?"

Randi immediately began to protest, but Sky interrupted her.

"Do you *want* to put on that dress? Do you *want* to try to move around a wagon and a campfire like that?"

Randi shook her head, "No, but—"

"But you're afraid of Violet's tongue again, aren't you?"

Randi nodded and grew red.

"You know what Violet's real problem is? She's jealous of you, Randi. You're pretty, and Violet doesn't like the competition." Sky began brushing her hair and rebraiding it for the day.

Randi picked up her brush and pulled it through her long brown strands. "Okay, I will. I think I'll wear my hair braided again too, instead of up like that lady told me I must. I've tried to fulfill my promise to my granddad, but if my future husband won't take me the way I am, I don't want him. And so far as pretty goes, you're the prettiest of all the women on this train, Sky. Violet is more jealous of you than she could ever be of me."

Sky laughed wickedly. "Let's really give Violet something to talk about. Do you know what a riding habit is?" Sky opened her trunk and dug down until she found what she was looking for. "The split-skirt is perfect for this kind of life." Her voice was muffled as she pulled something from the trunk. "I'll wear this blue one; Mother said it matched my eyes." Sky fluttered her eyes at Randi, causing her to giggle. "And you wear this brown one; it will be perfect with your hair. We'll just wear regular shirtwaists and leave off the jackets. What do you think?"

Randi fingered the fine material. "What if I tear it or burn it or..."

"So what?" Sky stopped her. "It's only a skirt. I have another whole trunk full of skirts and dresses. Please, Randi, do it for me." She looked beseechingly at her. "I can practice being a twin!"

Randi giggled again. "Okay, you win. I suppose I could put on my buckskins and really raise some eyebrows, but I'll start with this."

The girls stepped out of their wagon a short time later and headed for the stream with their buckets. Sky's long golden braid swung on her back, and her legs in the blue split skirt strode gracefully forward. Beside her, Randi mirrored her image with her own brown braid and split skirt. She marveled to Sky, "This skirt is wonderful; it's almost as nice as my buckskins! I feel more like myself than since I left Tennessee." Sky smiled at her friend's renewed self-confidence.

Hector rounded the corner just then with full buckets in his hands, and Randi's step faltered. At the sight of the two women, Hector stopped abruptly. The water in the buckets sloshed over onto his boots, and his mouth dropped open.

"Good morning, Mr. Riley," sang out Sky, but as they passed, she noticed that Hector's eyes followed Randi, and admiration shone from them. Then, as if remembering himself, he dropped the buckets, sending water flying everywhere, swept his hat off, and bowed to the women.

Randi giggled softly, and they continued on. Sky walked silently for a moment, glancing at her friend, before making up her mind to ask, "Do you like Hector, Randi?"

"Of course I like Hector. Everyone likes Hector Riley, except maybe Violet." Randi's face revealed nothing.

"But that's all?" Sky persisted. "I mean, you know you've agreed to marry another man, and it's not that Hector isn't nice or anything like that, but he is kind of clumsy and awkward and easily embarrassed around women... and—"

"He's not," interrupted Randi. She stopped and faced Sky, her teasing gone. "I'm not sure who Hector Riley is, but he is not *clumsy* or *awkward* or *embarrassed*." She stressed each word. "He's pretending, I think. I've...I've watched him...and when he doesn't think anyone is around, he's not like that at all."

"Then why—?"

"I don't know, but I'm sure he has a good reason." Randi started walking again.

"But Randi—" Sky took her arm. "You can't get involved with Hector if you're promised to someone else."

For a moment Randi's face was almost defiant. Then she shrugged. "I'm not. I won't. He's not interested in me anyway."

"Sky! Miranda!"

The girls turned as their names were called and saw Martha come running toward them.

"Morning, Sky. *Miranda?*" Martha looked Miranda up and down approvingly.

Sky's blue eyes sparkled. "I would like you to meet Randi Porter, Martha. Randi, this is my friend, Martha Scott." Sky jokingly made the introductions.

"Randi? Randi." Martha tried out the name. "You look wonderful, Randi! Good morning!" She smiled her pleasure before worry creased her brow again.

"Is there something wrong, Martha?" Randi asked.

"I don't know for sure, but I think there might be. Could you both eat breakfast with Angelina and me? I'll tell you more later."

At the girls' nods, Martha waved and left to go to her wagon.

"I wonder what that's all about," said Sky.

"I don't know, but trouble's up ahead," replied Randi softly.

Approaching were Violet and Gertie. Violet played with a handful of daisies while Gertie struggled with two buckets full of water. As Sky and Randi headed her way, Violet's eyes narrowed, and she glanced from one to the other, taking in every detail of their appearance.

"So the ball is over." She eyed the split-skirts with distaste. "And the cattle drive has begun. You know, girls, it's a good thing you have guaranteed husbands or you wouldn't have a chance dressed like that. Men like their women to be feminine." She twirled the flowers in her hand and smoothed her skirt.

Sky and Randi ignored her and kept walking to the stream. They dipped their buckets and started back, but

Violet was still waiting, hands on her hips. She faced Sky with a menacing look while Gertie stood nervously beside her.

"You're going to pay for your little performance last night, Miss High and Mighty," Violet hissed.

Sky again ignored her and continued to walk on by, but Violet's arm snaked out as Sky passed. She grabbed Sky's long braid and gave it a hard yank, but before Sky's head had a chance to snap back into place, Randi flipped her water bucket over Violet's head.

A scream of rage broke the stillness of the early morning. Sky broke out in helpless giggles as Violet threw the bucket and stood glowering at both of them. Water dripped from her hair, her nose, and her dress. She shivered in the cool breeze as Gertie stared in disbelief.

Randi calmly retrieved the bucket and dipped it into the stream again. She returned to Sky's side, the bucket held ready, and, smiling sweetly at Violet, said, "Would you like another rinse, or are you finished with your morning bath?"

Sky's giggles erupted into laughter, and Gertie tried to hide a smile.

Colonel Stultz and Mr. Dewell burst through the trees on a run, guns drawn. Hector bounded after them swiftly. His eyes swept over Randi and Sky before stopping on Violet. He looked back at Randi's stance and the threatening bucket, and he grinned.

"What happened? What's wrong?" The colonel held his gun ready and looked past the women toward the stream and into the surrounding trees. Mr. Dewell saw

Violet's condition and chuckled while he rubbed a hand over his mustache. He put away his gun.

"Looks like everything is under control, colonel. False alarm." His eyes flickered toward Violet, and the colonel followed with his own.

"Yes, yes I see. " The colonel cleared his throat. "Let's get back to breakfast, then."

"Just a minute, Mr. Dewell!" Violet pushed the dripping hair off her forehead. "There is something I think you'd better see." She flashed a look of triumph at Sky. "We have stowaways along. If you'd come look with me in Martha Scott's wagon, I'll show them to you."

Sky took a sharp breath and heard Randi's voice mutter something. Hector's expression was thunderous, and even Gertie looked at her friend in shock. The colonel was surprised, but knowing this would happen sooner or later, said nothing as Mr. Dewell asked,

"Stowaways? On our wagon train? What stowaways?"

Violet, enjoying center stage once again, strode forward and took the wagon master's arm. "If you'll just come with me, please."

She led the way with Mr. Dewell. The rest of the party stared after the couple for a moment; then Sky dropped her bucket and raced after them. The rest, except for Colonel Stultz, were propelled into motion and followed.

"Mr. Dewell, please let me explain." Sky caught up to them.

"I will make the explanations now," said Violet, glaring at Sky. "You can do nothing about this, Miss Hoffman. Martha Scott broke the rules, and you know it."

Martha and Angelina looked up as the group approached their wagon. The other ladies gathered around, made curious by the commotion.

Martha took in Violet's wet hair and dress and began, "Violet, what's happened to—?"

"Never mind that," Violet interrupted. She stopped dramatically at the back of the covered wagon and said, "Mr. Dewell, here are your stowaways." And she flipped open the covering.

"Violet, no!" Martha protested.

Mr. Dewell looked at Martha then into the wagon. A little boy sat beside a sleeping baby. At the sight of all the people, he began to cry.

The wagon master, puzzled, looked again at Violet and Martha; then he held out his arms to the boy and coaxed, "Come here, little fellow. Come see Uncle Dewey." The child crept out of the wagon into the older man's arms.

"There, there now. Everything is okay. Who's child is this?" he asked, looking at Martha.

"They are my children, Mr. Dewell." Martha spoke clearly, her back stiff. "I will not leave them behind, and I will not be put off this wagon train because of them. Is that clear?" Her hands belied her brave words as they nervously plucked at her apron. Violet looked smug.

"Well there's no reason you should be." The wagon master bounced the little boy in his arms and smiled at him. "Why wasn't I told there were children along? I love children. Me and this little fellow will have lots of fun together. Why ever did you try to hide them?"

"Well, I—" Martha began. She caught sight of Colonel Stultz slipping behind the wagons. "I guess I thought you didn't want children along on a wagon train," she said bitterly.

"Not want children?" Mr. Dewell laughed. "This wagon train business is hard, boring work. But children make it a lot more fun. They liven things up a bit, don't you think? No, I've taken lots of children on wagon trains. It can be a bit hard on the young babies, but yours in there doesn't look to be newborn, so he should be okay. I recollect a time when I was leading a wagon train out, and the night before we left a newborn baby was brought to one of the families from a midwife in the town. She said the mother gave birth to two babies and could only afford to keep one, so she gave the other to a family that had just lost theirs. What a time we had with that baby! Cried every night and nearly kept the whole camp awake. Now, yours, Mrs. Scott, must be an angel to be so quiet. I never even knew you had a baby along."

He chuckled as he ruffled the boy's hair. "No, I don't mind children at all. Now let's finish breakfast and get rolling. See you later, little fellow."

Sky's mouth was dry. Her heart thundered in her ears, and she barely heard Randi's excited voice saying,

"Sky! Doesn't that sound like your twin? Ask him, Sky. Ask him!"

Randi pushed her forward, and Sky caught up to the man. Swallowing her excitement she asked, "Mr. Dewell, wait, please."

The wagon master stopped again, tapping his foot. Clearly he was impatient to get underway after the morning's delays. "Yes?"

Sky cleared her throat and said, "That baby you were talking about. Do you remember how long ago it happened?" Her eyes followed as he pulled off his hat and scratched his balding head. "Please, sir, it's important!"

"Well now, I'm not sure what year that was. I've done this so often, I lose track, you know." Sky's eyes pleaded with him to remember. "I'd have to say eighteen, maybe twenty years ago, why?"

"Oh Mr. Dewell" Sky's eyes shone with excitement. "I think you're describing my twin sister. I have a letter from my mother telling me almost the same story, and it happened twenty years ago. Who were the people who took the baby?"

The old man's eyes softened with understanding. "Well, isn't that something? Imagine there being another girl as pretty as yourself, miss. Let me see." He pondered the problem a few moments while Sky stood by, dizzy with hope. "No, I just can't think what it was. There were so many. I remember the situation mostly because of the odd circumstances involved. I'll have to give it more thought, Miss Hoffman." He saw her defeated look.

"One thing I do remember. They were the kindest people I ever met. They loved that little baby even with all the crying." His brow creased again in thought. "They had other children too, I think, and the man, the father, led the Sunday services for the whole train. Good Christian people, they were." He smiled, pleased with the information he was able to give her.

Sky smiled. "Oh Mr. Dewell, thank you so much! Please, please try to remember their names."

"I will, miss. I'll keep working on it. It'll come to me." He backed away, embarrassed by the emotion he felt.

"Sky! It's a miracle!" Randi hugged her friend. "We'll pray that Mr. Dewell will remember that name."

"It is just too much to take in! My head is spinning." Sky laughed. "Just think; that man led the train my sister was on."

"I'm so happy for you, Sky, but we'd better see what Martha wanted before we roll today. She's waiting by her wagon." Randi led her in that direction. "Violet isn't going to stop trying to get even with you, you know. I think I understand her a little better now."

Sky stopped and studied her friend's face. She could think of no explanation for her comment. "What do you mean?"

"I overheard the colonel tell Mr. Dewell that she came straight to him from an orphanage. She'd lived in one all her life, even taught there when she got older because she couldn't find other work, apparently."

Sky shook her head sadly. It explained a lot about Violet, but it didn't excuse her behavior.

"Wasn't that mean of Colonel Stultz to make Martha hide her children from Mr. Dewell?"

Anger filled Sky as she remembered. "He lied to Martha deliberately. He just didn't want to bring a bride with children along because the prospective husbands might protest."

They reached Martha's side, and she agreed as she heard Sky's comment.

"I'm sure that was it, Sky, and that's the problem I wanted to talk to you about."

She took a deep breath then lowered her voice and said, "Angelina's been sick every morning since we left."

Both Sky and Randi looked bewildered. "Can we help? Is she all right? What's wrong with her?"

Martha looked from one woman to the next in exasperation and said, "She's pregnant."

Chapter 13

Sand Creek

The funeral was over. Evan stood by the graveside while the others slowly left. His throat was tight, and tears stung behind his eyelids. *Why, God?* he questioned. *Why someone young and full of life like Michael?*

His best friend and neighbor was dead, kicked by a horse. It was the kind of accident that could happen to anyone, at any time. The men like he and Michael, who were homesteading on their own, faced situations involving potential injury every day. Michael died alone in a field. *If someone had only been there,* thought Evan, *he might not have died.*

Michael would not want his friend to grieve over him. How often had he told Evan how he longed for heaven? He even said he looked forward to it more than to his mail-order bride.

His bride. Evan placed his hat back on his head. He'd have to get word to her. He looked down at the grave one more time.

"Good-bye for now, dear friend. I'll be seeing you again."

A week passed, and Evan found himself standing on the boardwalk waiting for the stage. It was too late to send word to Miss Ella Burkett, so he would have to tell her in person. He felt an obligation to Michael to be the one to inform his bride-to-be of his death and pay her way back home. He also felt protective of her well-being; there were men in the town who would gladly take Michael's place and were waiting around to get a look at the woman. Evan couldn't explain his feelings, but he somehow felt it was dishonorable for another man to take Michael's place too soon.

Evan shifted his feet. He was impatient to get back to his work. Most of his crops were in, but there was so much more he needed to do, and he had a wife on the way too. The thought didn't lift his spirits. The approach of the stagecoach made him look up.

Dust settled over the swaying coach as the driver stopped the team. The door opened and a portly man stepped out then turned and helped an elderly lady behind him. The only other passenger was a young woman.

Evan's heart leaped. She was a beauty! Under her hat he glimpsed blonde hair, neatly coiled. Her blue eyes found his, and her brows rose questioningly as Evan stepped forward and offered his hand.

"Are you Miss Ella Burkett?" he inquired. Her hand felt so small in his as her fingers gripped his for support.

"Yes, I am. Mr. Calloway?" A look of relief and hope passed over her face as she took in Evan's handsome features.

"No. I am, I *was* Michael Calloway's neighbor. My name is Evan Trent."

"I don't understand. Won't Mr. Calloway be in to meet me?" She withdrew her hand.

"Miss Burkett, there's no easy way to tell you this..." Evan rotated his hat brim in his hands and looked at his boots.

"He doesn't want me, does he? Is that it, Mr. Trent?" She almost seemed to have expected this turn of events.

"No, Miss Burkett. He wanted you very much. It was all he could talk about...you coming to be his bride." Evan hastened to reassure her. He paused, and Ella waited, puzzled.

"He died about a week ago, Miss Burkett. It was an accident there on his homestead, and I'm the one who found him."

"He's *dead*?" Ella was stunned. The coach driver set her bags on the boardwalk beside her, tipped his hat, and left. Ella looked blankly at the bags. Then, as realization sank in, she turned to Evan with a stricken look.

Evan's heart wrenched. He hated telling her so suddenly, but what could he do?

"I can't go back," Ella said. "I won't go back; there's nothing for me there." She spoke the words out loud, though Evan didn't think she'd meant to.

Evan reached down and picked up Ella's bags and set them inside the mercantile as he had arranged with Harry Nolan. He put his hand under her elbow and said, "How about if we get something to eat while we decide what to do next? I hope you don't mind, but the only eating place we have so far is the saloon. It's early enough that there won't be many there. Harry Nolan, one of the brothers who owns the mercantile, is planning to start a hotel and dining room..." He kept up a flow of words as they walked toward the saloon. Ella followed in a daze.

Evan was irritated by the men who stood around staring at Ella. Word was already out that she was in town. He thought Ella hadn't noticed, for she was quiet throughout their meal, not eating much and saying even less. While they were waiting for their coffee, she said, "I take it there aren't many women in this town?"

Evan glanced sharply at her and noticed that she was looking better. "No, ma'am. Most of us here are home-steaders, some are ranchers, some loggers. We're just get-ting this town established, so not many of us have wives yet. That's...that's why Michael sent for you." Evan strug-gled to find the right words. He wanted Ella to know the kind of man Michael was and to have her like him even though she would never know him. He continued, "He was a good man—"

He stopped as the door swung open and Bert Davies, the banker, rushed in. He spotted Evan with Ella and walked purposefully to them, sweeping off his hat as he approached. That he was excited and flustered at seeing the pretty woman was an understatement. His words came out in a rush.

"Welcome to our town, miss. My name's Bert Davies. I run the bank. We're all very happy to have a lovely lady like yourself here." He beamed at her all the while he was talking.

Evan was disgusted. "Bert, if you don't mind, we were just discussing Michael."

"Oh, yes! Good man, he was. It's really too bad about him dying. Awfully sorry, miss. Mind if I sit down?"

"Bert!" exclaimed Evan.

"Well, now, isn't this a shame." Ned Bolter sauntered over from the bar. "Here we have a woman looking for a husband"—he pointed to Ella, and she stared back in distaste—"and over here we have two men looking for wives, but they can't have *her*"—he pointed again—"because they signed contracts to marry someone else already!" He laughed mockingly at the men.

"Did you gents forget your brides are on the way? Unless, of course, the poor colonel has trouble getting them here." He laughed again and staggered back toward the bar. "But then he'll have me to deal with. Me and a rope." Bolter collapsed in a chair, laughing drunkenly.

Ella looked at the two men with questions in her eyes, and it was enough to make Bert Davies rise. He mumbled something as he excused himself.

"Miss Burkett, would you like me to take you to where you'll be staying?" Evan pushed back his chair and held hers while she stood. She gave him a grateful look.

"Where is it that I'll be staying?" she asked. A touch of uncertainty was in her voice.

They left the noise of the saloon behind them as they walked back down the boardwalk.

"Michael arranged for you to stay with the doctor and his wife until you were ready to...uh...to marry him." Evan stammered out the explanation. "They said you could stay as long as you need to. There's no hotel yet or boarding house, like I said." The doctor also told Evan that he didn't expect any unmarried female to remain unmarried long in this town. There would be callers, and for some reason Evan didn't like the idea.

"So tell me about this contract you and the others signed," said Ella. She glanced sideways at Evan.

Evan hesitated. Why was he reluctant to tell her about it? Was it because she had such incredibly long, dark eyelashes over those pretty blue eyes, or because he had caught just a glimpse of a dimple when she forgot her troubles a moment and smiled at something he'd said? He mentally shook himself. He had no business thinking these thoughts about his best friend's bride.

"Well, after talking my ear off, Michael convinced me that I needed a wife too. Colonel Stultz is the man we hired to find us wives." They reached the doctor's house and stood outside. "Twelve of us men put up two-thirds of the money, and we'll pay the final third when the colonel delivers." The explanation sounded stilted even to his ears, and he couldn't look at her as he spoke. He felt embarrassed to admit that he had ordered a bride, but he didn't know why. After all, he was talking to a mail-order bride.

"But what is this contract?" Ella persisted. She colored slightly, but Evan didn't notice. He was looking down at the bags he carried.

"The colonel insisted we all sign contracts promising to marry the women he brought here."

"Isn't that rather risky?" Ella dared ask. "I mean, at least I wrote to Michael Calloway and told him what I was like, and he wrote to me so I knew a little about who I was agreeing to marry." She looked up into Evan's face. "I'm sorry. That's none of my business."

"No, it's okay." Evan let out the breath he had been holding. "Actually I've been asking myself the same question. What have I done? What if I don't like her?" He looked into Ella's eyes. "What if she doesn't like me?" Their eyes held each other's gaze.

Ella broke away first, glancing down at her hands then back to Evan again.

"Is that the most important thing to you, that you like each other?"

Evan set the bags down and slowly straightened. "No," he spoke carefully, watching her face. "I mean, it's important, yes, but more importantly I want the woman I marry to know and love the LORD. I'd like to know that she had accepted Christ as her savior." He paused uncertainly a moment then plunged on. "That's what Michael wanted most too." Again he caught Ella's eyes. "Is that what he would have gotten?"

Ella's smile was sad. "Yes, I know the LORD. I became a Christian as a child. I have to admit that I was very unsure of becoming a mail-order bride because I didn't know if it was the right thing to do as a Christian. I didn't know if I should plan to marry a man I didn't know. But I felt so sure of the LORD leading me here, and Michael's letters seemed to answer all my questions. I could no longer stay where I was. I had no work and no husband. Now I come here, and right away a door is closed to my future. Why did God send me here and then have Michael die?" Her breath caught in a small gasp.

Evan reached out and took her arms. The gentle but firm pressure calmed her, and she blinked back her tears.

"I don't know what the LORD wants for you, Ella, but don't give up on him. Trust him; he'll continue to lead you. He cares more than we realize."

The door of the house opened, and Evan let his hands drop from her arms. The doctor's wife looked from one to the other then said, "You must be Miss Burkett. Evan, bring the girl in. Don't keep her standing out there for all the men to gawk at."

The two approached, and at Ella's uncertain look the doctor's wife held out her arms and enveloped her in a comforting hug.

"You've had quite a day, haven't you, deary? Come along, and we'll get you settled."

Ella turned back to Evan and held out her hand.

"Thank you, Mr. Trent. Thank you for supper and for your kindness." She looked him in the eye as she added, "I wish the best to you and your bride."

Evan's heart felt heavy as he took her hand and murmured good-bye. He turned to go and bumped into the doctor entering his home.

"Evan! Good to see you." The doctor smiled and shook hands. "Is this our new boarder?" He smiled and took Ella's hands and said, "You are beautiful, my dear. A lovely addition to our home, isn't she, Florrie?" He looked to his wife. "You're welcome to stay as long as you like."

Ella shook her head. "But I can't," she said. Despair sounded in her voice. "I have no money to pay you. Unless..."—she looked from Evan to the doctor—"unless you know where I might get a job?"

Evan started to speak. He'd hire her to do something, anything, but the doctor beat him to it.

"I thought you might feel that way, Miss Burkett, and I only hope you will agree to what I propose. I need help. The men in this town are more inclined to injuries than anyplace I've ever been, and I'm busy all the time. Would you consider being my helper?" He smiled kindly at her. "And may I call you Ella?" he added.

Relief washed over Ella's face, and she looked like a burden had been lifted from her heart. Evan was startled again by her beauty when she smiled back at the doctor.

"I would like that very much, sir. I've helped with sick people before, but you'll have to teach me a lot, I'm sure. But I'm a fast learner," she hastened to add. Her eagerness was contagious, and they all smiled.

Evan nodded to the group again then looked at Ella and said, "Then I'll be seeing you again, Miss Burkett. Good night."

"Good night, Mr. Trent," Ella said softly. As her eyes followed him out the door, the doctor and his wife exchanged glances.

Ella's eyes closed in a silent prayer, *Lord, show me what to do next.*

Chapter 14

Train

Smythe bent over and presented the cigar case to his employer. Rudolph Hadley selected one and handed it back to his man to prepare for him.

The detective sat nervously across from Hadley on the moving train. Hadley was not an easy man to deal with, but he paid well.

"We believe Miss Hoffman took this train to the end of its run at Leaf River," the detective reported as he checked his notebook. "I had one of my men check at each stop, but he was told that no one of her description got off. Someone is lying, because Miss Hoffman did not return on the train." The man flipped ahead a few pages.

"There are stage coach lines along the way that I have men checking on now. The only other possibility I can offer is that a wagon train left from the last stop shortly after the train would have gotten there. It was headed for the northern regions, some new settlement called Sand Creek in Minnesota."

Hadley's face showed no expression, so nervously the detective continued, "I have my doubts that Miss Hoffman would have joined that wagon train, sir. It was a group of women who were going as brides for the men of Sand Creek."

"Brides?" Hadley queried.

"Yes, sir. I suppose it sounds odd to you, but these frontier lands can be pretty wild. Usually the men go out on their own and set up homesteads or start prospecting. When a place gets established and people want to stay on, the men sometimes advertise for wives to join them there. Sometimes it works; sometimes it doesn't."

"Barbaric country," commented Hadley. He puffed on his cigar and blew out the smoke in carefully spaced intervals. Would Sky join a train of brides? He couldn't picture her becoming someone's wife that easily. No, but she might use the wagon train for transport.

"I want that wagon train investigated. I want names of all the women traveling to this Sand Creek. Send someone on ahead to the town too. Have him telegraph any information he learns."

"There's no telegraph there yet, sir," said the detective. As Hadley stared at him, he shifted position on the seat and continued. "I can send a man out there, but he'd have to travel to the next nearest town to send back a report. It would take some time, and she might not even be with that wagon train."

"Do it," commanded Hadley. "And have the train investigated while it's on its way. I think we'll head in that direction ourselves. I have a hunch about this."

The detective frowned slightly. This was going to take time, but if the rich gent was willing to pay, why not? "Yes, sir. I'll send instructions to my men at the next stop."

Chapter 15

Wagon Train

Sky bounced on the wagon seat as she drove the oxen, and Miranda walked close by so the two could talk without anyone nearby hearing.

"Do you think Martha is right about Angelina?" Randi asked. "She does look like she's not feeling well."

"And she looks so sad too," added Sky. She gritted her teeth as the wagon rolled up another rock and landed with a thud. Mr. Dewell was taking them over a rough trail today. How she wanted to trade places with Randi and stretch her legs! But she'd stick it out; she owed it to Randi for the many days she'd done it for her.

Sky saw amusement on Randi's face. "I can drive if you're getting tired, Sky." Randi hid a smile.

"It's not the driving that tires me." Sky laughed. "It's the riding. No, I'll manage. Enjoy your walk. Tomorrow it is your turn again." She was amazed that even though she had been brought up prim and proper, she was adapting quite readily to this more rugged lifestyle.

"We'll be eating with Martha and Angelina again tonight. Maybe we can find out more and help Angelina if she's willing." Randi looked concerned. "It'll be rough for a woman in her condition."

"What do you know about...about that?" asked Sky. She was embarrassed. She'd never talked about pregnancies before.

"I was present at several birthings when we were with the Indians," Randi stated matter-of-factly. "I've also helped with horses and cattle. It's a wonderful thing. I always marvel at God's miracle of life. But Angelina won't even be close to delivering while we're traveling, if she really is with child. And after she gets over the sickness, she should handle the rest of the trip just fine. I was thinking of when we get to the town. Will a man want her and a baby on the way?"

Sky hadn't thought of that. "You think that's why Colonel Stultz didn't want Martha and her children? He's afraid no one will want them?"

"It's possible," said Randi. "The Indians are different. They take in other children willingly, even white children. But I've seen white families refuse to take in orphaned children. They send them to orphanages to get rid of them." Randi's face was bitter, and Sky looked at her in surprise.

Randi saw the look and explained. "Before my grand-dad could come and get me, I was in one. I was only two years old, but I can still remember the feelings I had there." She shuddered.

Sky changed the subject. "Did you get a chance to look for tracks by our rock?"

Randi nodded. "I'm puzzled, Sky. They were made by someone in moccasins, but for some reason I can't explain, I don't think it was an Indian."

After supper was over and the women were relaxing after Janet's Bible reading, Sky and Randi learned that Angelina was indeed expecting a baby.

Angelina held Martha's little one cradled in her arms and stroked the soft face as she explained, "Ben said he loved me and wanted to marry me. We picked a date for our wedding and everything was going along so well. I loved him so much; I would have done anything for Ben, and I thought he felt the same way.

"When I told him I suspected we had a baby on the way, he changed. He started avoiding me. I thought everything would be all right since we were going to get married anyway. I just figured we'd marry sooner.

"About a week after I told Ben about the baby, I was walking down the street, and the storekeeper's wife stopped me and said, 'Did you hear the news? Ben Ford and Lila Peterson just tied the knot! They're at the preacher's house now.'

"I looked over at the house and saw Ben walking out with Lila on his arm. She had a bouquet of flowers in her hand. Ben saw me and looked away. I found the ad for brides and left the next day."

Angelina put her head down and sobbed quietly. Sky put her arms around the weeping woman, and Martha gently took the baby from her arms.

"I'm just like Janet says," sobbed Angelina. "I'm wicked and sinful, and I deserve to be sick and miserable as God's punishment. I deserve to die."

Sky looked bewildered, but Randi took over calmly. "Yes, you are wicked and sinful," she said gently. Sky looked at Randi in shock. "But so am I, Angelina, and so are Martha and Sky. No one on this earth is without sin. What you did was wrong, but we've all done wrong, too. We are no better and no worse than you."

Sky's eyes were uncertain as she watched Randi. Surely what Angelina had done was worse than anything Sky could think of having done. What was Randi trying to say?

"Angelina, you know that Jesus Christ died on the cross to pay for all sin." Randi spoke comfortingly, yet her voice demanded attention, and Angelina looked up.

"Yes," she answered.

"Let me repeat that," said Randi, looking Angelina in the eye. "He died and rose again to pay for *all* sin, right?"

"Yes," Angelina whispered, wiping off her wet face. She searched Randi's face closely.

"Then if all the sin we have ever done is paid for and all the sin we will ever do is paid for, what makes you think God hasn't paid for this sin too? You see, Angelina, we no longer live under the law system. We live under grace now. In Ephesians 3, the Apostle Paul explains how the gospel of the grace of God was delivered to him by God to give out to us. Today we are saved by grace alone through faith, apart from works."

"I know what you're saying," said Angelina. "I accepted Christ's death, burial, and resurrection for my salvation when I was a child. But I sinned as a Christian. I knew better. Janet says—"

"I know what Janet says," interrupted Randi. "She says God will judge you for your sins. Angelina, God has already judged your sin and paid for it. He did it on the cross. And just as we are saved by faith, we are told in God's Word that we should walk by faith. Our God is loving and kind, just as a father is to his own children. No sin can separate you from God. God forgives you, Angelina, because of Jesus Christ."

"But won't he punish me?"

"There are consequences to sin," said Randi. "You will live the rest of your life with a son or daughter to remind you. But it isn't punishment that God sends us; it's forgiveness, love, and help to go on, and that is what your child will be. A reminder that God isn't mean. You can learn from this and grow closer to God because of it. That's what he wants."

"He is a great and loving God," added Martha.

Sky was silent. She didn't understand any of this.

"Other people may scorn you, and you may be in for some rough times ahead, but God will never leave your side, and he will not condemn you. He offers you his love."

"What about my baby?" asked Angelina. "What if my baby dies when it is time for the birthing? Will my baby go to hell because of me? Janet says we're all born on the road to hell." Tears filled her eyes once again.

Randi spoke tenderly, "No, Angelina. Remember? Jesus Christ paid for *all* sin. My granddad helped me understand like this. He said since Christ paid the way to heaven for all people, we're all born into this world with the ticket to heaven in our hands. All the sin is out of the way in God's eyes. We can all go, but we all need to make the decision to believe in Jesus Christ as the 'ticket.' The only reason people go to hell is that they refuse to accept the ticket. They won't accept that Jesus Christ paid the way for them. They try to pay their own way instead by doing good works or being religious."

Randi took Angelina's hand. "Your baby has the ticket. The LORD Jesus made sure of that. And so do you. Have you accepted it?" Angelina nodded; then she reached out and hugged Randi.

"Thank you. You don't know how much you've helped me. I feel so much better."

"Good!" said Martha. "A happy mother makes a happy baby." She laughed. "We'll take good care of you on this trip, little mother."

Sky looked at the smiling women. Was becoming God's child that simple? She wasn't sure. She knew very little about the relationship between a father and child. The baron certainly had never been a father to her. She could only imagine what her life would have been like had her real father lived. But being *God's* child? That was something she needed to think about.

Chapter 16

Wagon Train

"I think since we've come this far, we have a right to know who our husbands are going to be," Violet spoke up at the evening meal.

Several women around the campfire nodded in agreement, but Sky saw others—quiet Nola, Belle's wagonmate, and especially Randi—look uncomfortable. She wasn't sure that she wanted to know, either.

"We should get to know something about them," agreed Bridget. "I've been a-dreaming of my man all this time, thinking he will be a tall one with black hair. Maybe I'll end up with a short, bald one!" She laughed. "Whichever way it is, I want to know."

"And he's probably dreaming of a quiet, peaceful woman, and has no idea of the talker he's about to get," added Gretchen.

"I hope we'll be able to live close to each other," Bridget said seriously, her teasing aside. The sisters looked at one another, and Gretchen smiled.

"I'll make sure of it," she said.

Sky enjoyed watching the sisters. The O'Donnells were as close to twins as she had ever seen.

"I'm going to ask the colonel about it now." Violet stood and brushed off her skirt. The colonel was just walking into the wagon circle, followed by Mr. Dewell and Hector. Crane was on guard duty.

"Colonel Stultz! We...all of us"—Violet waved her hand at the others—"demand to know who our husbands are going to be. You certainly have had plenty of time to match us up, haven't you?"

The colonel rubbed a hand over his goatee. He had been dreading this moment. He'd sat many evenings in his wagon going through the papers, trying to sort out who should marry whom. He thought it would be so simple to read what each man was looking for and match him to a woman. But they weren't matching up well. Finally he'd just picked a paper from the men's pile and picked a paper from the women's pile and put them together. He hoped that would work out.

Hector and Mr. Dewell filled their plates and sat down to eat. Hector watched the colonel with interest.

"Yes, you ladies are quite right. It is time to reveal your husbands to you and let you become better acquainted with them before you meet them in person." The colonel wiped his forehead with his handkerchief. "Warm tonight, isn't it! I'll get the papers from my wagon."

The women began whispering, and excitement grew. Sky shifted position nervously and glanced over at Randi. She was twisting her hands in her lap, refusing to look up. Sky noticed Hector look at Randi then look away, trying not to show his interest.

I don't know how Randi could become interested in Hector. He's good and kind, but so clumsy. And that hair! Sky's thoughts were interrupted by the colonel's return. He carried several papers in his hand, and the women quickly quieted.

The colonel looked over at Hector and Mr. Dewell, who were eating their supper. His stomach growled. "I don't suppose you care to wait until I've had my meal, would you? No, I suppose not," he added quickly as he looked at the faces before him. Relenting, he assumed an authoritative air.

"Ladies, as I promised, I have put time and consideration into making the perfect matches for each of you. My system worked beautifully, and I think you will all be pleased."

Some of the women leaned forward in eagerness; others seemed to shrink back.

"First, I have the O'Donnells."

Gretchen and Bridget stood up and walked toward the colonel. Bridget smiled excitedly, and she held out a hand to Gretchen, who smiled tolerantly at her sister, but she, too, seemed nervous.

"I have found a perfect match for the two of you," said the colonel. He felt he was safe on this one. He held out a paper to each of them. "The Nolans are brothers who run the mercantile of Sand Creek."

Bridget squealed in delight. "Brothers, Gretchen! We'll be living close to each other for sure." Gretchen looked relieved.

"Naturally," continued the colonel, pleased with his first success, "I matched the older brother, Jonas, with Gretchen, and Harry, the younger brother, with you, Miss Bridget."

"Harry. Harry Nolan. Bridget Nolan. Mrs. Harry Nolan." Bridget rattled off the names. Gretchen smiled at her sister and, calmly taking her arm, led her back to their wagon.

Colonel Stultz brightened. This wasn't going too badly. "Next I have Martha Scott." He smiled over at the woman. Martha handed her baby to Angelina, and, taking her son's hand, she walked up to the colonel. The boy tugged at his mother's hand, and when she saw what he wanted, she let him go with a smile. He raced over to "Uncle Dewey" and climbed up on his legs. The wagon master laughed and bounced him on his knee.

"Mrs. Scott, I believe I've found you the perfect husband. I have a man here who says he wants lots of children." He handed her the paper with a smile.

"But will he accept someone else's children?" she asked in a quiet voice. She took the paper and returned to Angelina's side.

The colonel looked after her. She should be grateful; it was good of him to bring her along with her children in the first place.

Sky watched anxiously as he proceeded to match Nola with a farmer, Bertha with a barber, and Belle with a blacksmith. Belle was delighted!

"Oh good! That means I'll be living in town. There will be people I can visit with, and maybe we'll be neighbors." She smiled at the O'Donnells, and they looked pleased too.

The colonel shuffled through his papers. He was getting hungrier as he smelled the food being kept warm over the fire. He'd have to speed this up. "Now for Miranda Porter and Sky Hoffman," he called out.

The two rose together and started forward. Hector stood up at the same time, and Sky and Randi hesitated as he stepped past them on the way to the campfire. He bent over the fire and picked up the coffee pot. The handle was obviously too hot to touch, and he dropped the pot with a crash, scattering red coals and hot liquid. He lost his balance and fell forward narrowly missing the fire, but he caught himself by grabbing on to the colonel's legs. The heavyset colonel teetered one way then another. His hands flew up into the air to aid his balance, and the pile of papers left his arms, spiraled into the air, and dropped gracefully into the fire.

The entire camp was silent for a heartbeat, then the colonel exploded, "Riley, you fool! Let go of me!" Hector released his hold on the colonel's legs, and both men fell in a heap. The colonel groaned.

Violet screamed and raced to the fire. "They're burning! Someone get them out. Quick!" She took a stick and tried to pull the papers from the flames, but it was too late. The pages curled and blackened in seconds.

"You idiot!" she screamed at Hector. She started toward him with the stick raised like a club in her hands.

Randi stepped forward in one fluid movement and gripped Violet's arm with her hand. She squeezed, and Violet whimpered and dropped the stick. She glared at Randi while she rubbed her arm.

"Don't you realize what that stupid fool has done?" She looked at the others. "Now we won't know! We'll have to wait until we get there. It's not fair!"

Many others looked as angry as Violet, but Sky and Randi only felt relief.

The colonel disentangled himself from Hector's arms and legs and painfully stood up. Hector stood also and began brushing himself off by pounding his hat against his legs. Dust rose, causing the colonel to cough.

"For goodness sake, Riley! Stop that and go sit down!" Colonel Stultz's face was red as he shouted at the younger man. Hector meekly returned to his seat. He picked up his empty cup and looked longingly back at the coffee pot laying on its side. He started to rise.

"Don't even think about it," warned Janet Conly, shaking a long spoon at him. She stood guard by the fire and glared at Hector.

"Now what are we going to do, colonel?" Violet demanded. "You must remember who you matched the rest of us up with."

He didn't. He only had a list of the men's names and what they still owed him. A list of names and a box of photographs wasn't going to do much good. The photographs!

"Please, ladies!" The colonel held up his arms, straining the buttons on his shirt. "I think I can satisfy your curiosity. I'm sorry about the papers"—he glared at Hector, who hung his head—"but I have something you might like even better. I have photographs of your husbands-to-be."

Excited chattering erupted as he left and returned with a box. The women impatiently watched him. He picked up one of the photographs, turned it over, turned it over again, studied it, then a peculiar expression crossed his face. "The only problem is that I don't know which face goes to which name." He looked apologetically at the women. "They aren't labeled."

"You mean we'll have a picture, but we won't know who he is or what he does until we get there?" asked Janet.

The colonel scratched his head. "I think I can remember a couple," he said, "but the rest...yes, that's the way it will have to be." He looked sheepish.

"Well, it's better than nothing," said Janet. "Which ones do you remember?"

The colonel looked through the photographs one by one. Some tried to gather around for a look, but he waved them back.

"Wait, please. Give me time."

This wasn't going to be easy. He hadn't paid much attention to the way the men looked. He was interested in their money. Out of the twelve pictures, he could place only four men.

"Okay." He took a deep breath, and the women waited anxiously. "Riley, you stay right there. Don't move!"

Hector looked hurt.

"I know which two are the Nolan brothers. They look enough alike that it wasn't too difficult." He held out the two photographs for the O'Donnells.

Bridget rushed up and grabbed them. "Oooh! They're handsome, Gretchen. Which one is Harry and which is Jonas?"

The colonel shrugged.

"This is the blacksmith," the colonel said next. "I remember because he was the biggest man there."

Belle walked forward and took the picture. She smiled nervously then laughed.

"He looks nice!" she said and showed the curious ladies.

"And this one's the barber. I remember him because he was the last one, and his hair is combed so neatly." Bertha claimed the picture.

"Now there's eight left. How do we do this?" He was unsure.

Ever the organizer, Janet took over. "We'll have to form a line, oldest to youngest. Otherwise we'll be fighting over these stupid pictures. Does everyone agree?"

Sky shrugged. Randi said nothing. The others all agreed except for Violet.

"That's not fair! Most of you are older than me. I'll be one of the last ones."

"I think you would be in the middle either way. Now line up."

Janet would have made a good officer in an army, thought Sky. She let Janet place her in line.

Nola went first. Even though the colonel had given her a paper, she didn't know which picture it matched. Someone else might pick out the picture of the man on her paper, so she threw the paper into the fire with the others and went to choose a photograph.

Janet was next, followed by Martha, who also discarded her paper. Then it was Sky's turn.

I don't even care, she thought. *I should let the others choose and then just take what's left.*

Then she saw a heavily bearded man with long hair in one of the photos, and she shuddered. She didn't want him!

I better pick someone I think I might like anyway, she decided.

There was a smiling, handsome face, and she reached for the photograph. It was snatched from her fingers by Violet.

"This one's mine! I saw him first." And she hurried off with it.

Sky looked after the fleeing girl angrily then shrugged. She picked up the next photo, aware that the others were getting impatient behind her.

The picture was blurred, as if the man had moved just before it was taken. Gertie crowded her, and Randi and Angelina were waiting, so Sky took the blurry picture and sat down.

Randi joined her in a moment. She was holding a picture, but she wasn't looking at it. Sky followed her gaze, and she saw Hector disappear behind the wagons. She looked back at Randi.

"What does yours look like?" she asked.

Randi held out the picture. Sky was taken aback. The man in Randi's photograph had an insolent look on his face as if he was making fun of the photographer.

"There were only two left, so I let Angelina choose before me. The man she picked didn't look much better than this one. He didn't even have a collar and tie on. But she said there was something about him that she liked. I don't know how she could tell anything about him; he was all hair and beard."

"Here's mine. Not much to see, is there?" Sky showed Randi the blurred picture.

At least all this is taking me in the right direction, she thought. *I'm getting closer to finding my twin. If only Mr. Dewell could remember the name of that family.*

A few nights later, Sky took a solitary stroll around the wagons. Randi was helping Martha get her children ready for the night.

Sky needed to think. She had to make some decisions about her future. Her skirt swished softly in the grass in rhythm to her strides. The night's dampness was settling in, and she rubbed her arms against the chill as she thought.

First on her mind was what Randi had told her about God. Sky twisted her hands in the folds of her skirt while she considered the incredible statements Randi had made.

I guess I've always known I'm a sinner; I'm certainly no saint, but I'm not that bad. She thought about Angelina and what she had done. *Randi says God sent Jesus to pay for what Angelina did and for what I have done and still may do.* Sky shook her head, disturbed by this thought. She hadn't been to church since she was a little girl. Her mother stopped going early on, being disillusioned with her life and marriage to the baron. So Sky didn't have a religious background. All she had ever really believed—when she thought about it—was that her goodness would eventually outweigh her badness and God would let her into heaven. But that's not what Randi had shown her in the Bible.

It was getting cooler, and Sky shivered in the night air while her thoughts moved on to her next pressing issue.

I've agreed to marry a man I've never met! How did I get myself into this? She pondered the problem then ticked the reasons off on her fingers.

My money is gone. Rudolph Hadley has detectives looking for me. I need to get to Minnesota to find my sister. This wagon train is the only safe way out of town. I have to become a bride to ride with it.

She walked in silence while hopelessness enveloped her.

I am dependent on this wagon train for my survival, and unless I can get a job in Sand Creek, I will be forced to marry to survive.

But I'm being forced anyway. I signed legal papers agreeing to this marriage.

She stopped and considered that fact, and determination and pride filled her.

I will honor the contract! I will keep my word. I only hope my husband will allow me to continue my search for my sister. I'm getting so close—

Her thoughts were interrupted when she heard voices. Men's voices. She looked around her and realized she had walked farther from the wagons than she should have. Who else could be this far from camp? Sky felt alarm, but she stood very still so as not to make her presence known.

"Boy, it's great to see you again! How've you been? Taken any bullets lately?"

"Nope. I'm too fast for them. What's the deal with the wagon train?"

"Bunch of mail-order brides going to a place called Sand Creek."

"Mail-order brides? Heard something about them. Must be some desperate females to agree to doing that! Couldn't get a husband any other way, I suppose. Do I really have to meet up with them tomorrow?" There was a false whining in his voice as he joshed with the other man.

Laughter followed. Sky held her breath as her heart raced painfully in her chest. The voices seemed familiar, but she could not place them.

"You *better* show up tomorrow. We've got preparations to make before the others arrive. See you then."

Sky quickly crouched down to hide as one man headed toward the wagons. She peeked through the bushes, but he was gone.

Chapter 17

Wagon Train

"All I'm trying to say is that one of the men from this wagon train is not who he pretends to be. I didn't say it was Hector." Sky tried to calm a ruffled Randi. The women were both riding so they could talk without being overheard by the others. Sky continued to relate what she had heard the previous night.

"The funny thing is...*both* voices were familiar, but I just can't place who they were. We need to watch for the man who comes into the camp today. He's sure to give away the other man."

"What do you think they meant about 'making preparations before others arrived'?" asked Randi. "What's going on?"

Sky didn't know. She was visibly shaken by the event, and when Randi told her that she'd be praying, Sky could only hope that Randi had a good enough connection with

God to get the results she wanted. She turned the conversation back to Hector.

"Why are you so defensive of Hector anyway? You aren't seriously interested in him, are you?"

Randi squirmed on the seat. She glanced sideways at her new friend, and Sky saw a blush stain the younger woman's face.

"You really are! Are you in love with him?"

"Sky!" Randi looked around to see how close they were to the other wagons. "Keep your voice down, please!"

As Sky continued to stare at her, Randi finally spoke.

"Hector is really quite nice. I've…I've been watching him, and you don't realize it, Sky, but he's a real gentleman. I've seen him carry water for Belle and haul wood for Nola. He even scrubbed a pot for Janet although he was soaked through by the time he was done." Randi laughed. "Not that he needed to be," she added softly.

Sky's eyebrows creased together as she frowned. "What do you mean?"

But Randi ignored the question. "And he picked me these." She shyly pulled a small bouquet of crushed daisies from her skirt pocket.

Sky's expression changed to astonishment. "He likes you too! But, Randi—*Hector?*"

Randi shrugged. "There's more to Hector Riley than he's letting on," she said mysteriously. "I guess I am sweet on him," she admitted.

"But what about—" Sky began then stopped. No need going over this marriage contract again.

Shy again, Randi questioned Sky. "Have you ever been sweet on anyone?"

Sky stared blankly at her a moment then looked straight ahead. She was surprised that the image of the man who had helped her in New York flashed in her mind. She didn't even know him!

"I don't...I don't think so," she murmured. But there he was with his dark hair and his cowboy hat and his strong arms, and again she relived how he "rescued" her.

Randi saw the dreamy look on her companion's face and wondered.

Sky and Randi were in charge of the cooking again at the next evening meal. The usual venison stew was seasoned with Randi's special talents, and even Sky earned compliments on her fluffy biscuits. The food had all been served, and Sky had just sat down to eat hers when a voice called from outside the circle.

"Hello the camp!"

Sky jumped, and Hector and Mr. Dewell reached for their guns as a man walked between two wagons and entered the circle.

"Got any coffee for a traveler?" he asked pleasantly. He wore a gun on his hip, but he kept his hands clear to show the men he meant no harm.

"What do you want, stranger?" asked Mr. Dewell.

"Smelled the food as I was passing and just couldn't resist it." The stranger smiled. "I've been riding the trail now for two weeks. Name's Rex Newton." Russ Newly introduced himself using the fake name he always used in his business. He waited patiently until Mr. Dewell lowered his gun.

"You're welcome to some supper, and we'll be glad to swap news with you, but after that you'll have to be on your way, Mr. Newton."

"Thank you, sir. I appreciate it."

Sky sat stunned. One of the voices from last night—it was his! And now she knew why it sounded familiar. He was the stranger who had saved her from Rudolph Hadley in New York! *Him!* What were the chances that they would meet again in the northwest wilderness? Was he working for Hadley somehow? She watched closely as he shook hands with Hector, Mr. Dewell, and Colonel Stultz.

Hector led Rex Newton to the campfire.

"Miss Hoffman and Miss Porter make some fighty mine stew. I...I mean, mighty fine stew." Hector stumbled over his words.

Russ Newly's eyebrows shot up at hearing the names. "Miss Hoffman?" He said the name out loud. His eyes searched for Sky among the women and, upon seeing her blue eyes staring at him, he appeared stunned. He strode to her and swept off his hat; his surprise was genuine.

"Miss Hoffman! How nice to see you again."

Sky felt pleasure tingle through her as she met the handsome man's eyes again. But she was wary. Something was not right here.

"Nice to see you too, Mr. Newton, is it?"

He nodded; then, although Sky didn't think he meant to, he asked, "What are you doing on a train like this?"

"A train like what?" responded Sky quickly.

Something flickered in Rex's eyes as he continued. "A train way out here in the wilderness. The last time I saw you, you were in the big city of New York. Quite a difference, wouldn't you say?"

Across the campfire Randi dipped stew onto the plate Hector held out. She watched Sky talking to the stranger while she also tried to unobtrusively watch Hector's behavior around the man.

Hector balanced the plate carefully and headed for Rex Newton. Sky saw him coming up behind Newton and held her breath, not knowing what catastrophe would ensue. Stew dripped off the side of the plate with each step Hector took.

Rex saw Sky look past him and curiously swung around to see what she was looking at. His sudden movement startled Hector, who stopped abruptly, and the stew sloshed forward, splattering Rex's shirtfront.

Rex threw up his arms to protect himself from the deluge, and Hector jumped back, thinking the man was going to strike him. The remaining stew sloshed down his own shirt and pants.

Mr. Dewell covered his eyes with one hand while Colonel Stultz sputtered, "Riley!" The colonel looked in exasperation between Hector and the wagon master.

In a choked voice, Mr. Dewell ordered, "Go relieve Crane now, Riley. And try to get cleaned up, or you'll attract skunks to the camp tonight."

Hector sheepishly looked at Sky and Randi before heading out of the wagon circle. A new voice hailing the camp stopped him, and he spun around with his gun in hand in one smooth, fluid motion. No one but Randi seemed to notice this unusual change in his actions.

Mr. Dewell rose again with his gun ready, and Rex Newton curiously watched while he devoured a fresh plate of stew.

Another man walked into the camp. This one was older than Rex and dusty from travel.

Sky was surprised because he looked familiar to her too. But how could that be? She only recently came to this country. Then with a small gasp, she slid between two of the wagons and pressed her back against one while she listened intently.

Rex and Randi both looked after her then back to the man. Randi casually walked to where Sky was hiding and leaned against the side of the wagon, her back to Sky.

Quietly she asked, "What's wrong, Sky? Who is he?"

Sky whispered back frantically, "It's that detective who was looking for me in Leaf River. He works for Rudolph Hadley!" Sky had told Randi about the man.

"Stay calm and be still," ordered Randi. "We won't let anything happen to you."

The detective walked toward the fire and helped himself to some stew with the wagon master's permission. He sat down to eat, and his eyes studied each of the women as he made conversation with Mr. Dewell and the colonel.

Rex joined the men, and Sky could see that Hector stayed by the wagons, watching. The other women sat or stood where they had been and watched the newcomers curiously. No one else seemed to notice that Sky had disappeared.

"Where you headed, mister?" Mr. Dewell asked the older man. Rex, for the moment, had been forgotten.

The detective chewed his mouthful of stew while he took another look around then replied, "I'm headed right here. I'm a detective; name's Conners. I'm working for an Englishman, name of Hadley."

Rex Newton's eyes hardened as he watched the man.

"He sent me to find a woman named Sky Hoffman. Now I've tracked her as far as Leaf River, the town this wagon train came from. It's my guess she's here." He looked intently at each of the men, yet watched for responses from the women. He wasn't disappointed. Angelina and Martha looked at each other worriedly, Janet gasped, Belle's hand went to her mouth, and Violet's head snapped up, her eyes bright with interest.

"There's no one here by that name!" Colonel Stultz declared. He wasn't about to give up any of the women.

The detective looked at the colonel through narrowed eyes.

Violet approached the man with a smile on her face. Mr. Dewell, the colonel, Hector, and Rex all watched helplessly as she asked, "Why? Is she wanted by the law? What did she do?"

"She's not wanted by the law, ma'am. I'm only a detective working for a private party. And as far as I know, she's done nothing wrong. The man just wants her located and returned to him. Now will you tell me where I can find her?"

Violet was thoroughly enjoying herself. She was finally going to pay Sky back and get rid of her too. "Oh, she's here all right," she said. The men scowled their disgust. "Why don't you ask Miss Porter where she's hiding?"

They all looked to where Randi had been standing, but she was gone.

Conners rose and headed in the direction they were looking. He stopped as Rex drew and pointed a gun at him. Mr. Dewell's gun covered his back.

"What makes you think the lady wants to go with you?" Rex demanded.

"I'm just doing my job, son. You've no call to draw a gun on me."

"No one leaves this train unless it's of their own free will," announced Mr. Dewell.

"And...and Miss Hoffman is under contract to remain with this train and marry...a man in Sand Creek, " sputtered the colonel.

Tension rose as Conners faced the three men. Finally he conceded. "Okay, gentlemen. If I can't bring her back with me, at least I can let my employer know that she has been located and—"

A piercing scream cut off his words.

The men and women turned as one to the sound. Hector leaped into action, yelling as he passed between the wagons, "The river!"

Rex followed with Conners close at his heels. Mr. Dewell shouted for the women to take cover as he checked his weapons and ammunition. Col. Stultz crouched behind a rock.

Hector and Rex reached the river first. They approached cautiously, guns drawn, but no one was in sight.

Conners panted heavily behind them as the two younger men studied the ground in the failing light.

"What is it?" he asked between gasps.

Hector jumped to his feet. "Indians." He pointed to the tracks. "Looks like half a dozen, probably a hunting party." He and Rex turned and headed back to the camp at a swift pace.

"What was the scream?" called Conners as he struggled to keep up.

Through clenched teeth Hector answered, "They took Randi and Sky!"

Chapter 18

Wilderness

Terror gripped Sky's throat, but she didn't let another scream escape. Her neck was still red from the Indian's fingers as he squeezed off her windpipe, nearly suffocating her.

As soon as Sky had heard Violet admit to the detective that she was with the train, she had fled. Randi overtook her and tried to calm her down.

They stood by the river debating what to do when, without warning, the Indians came. Sky heard no sound, but Randi swung around just as the nearest Indian reached her. At the sight of the nearly naked, painted man, Sky screamed, and his fingers closed on her throat.

She blacked out for a time, and when the fuzziness dissipated she was aware of being carried over the shoulder of one of the Indians. They were running as swiftly as they could, and she could see that Randi was in the same predicament behind her.

Sky began to struggle. Anything to slow them down! The Indians stopped immediately, and one pulled a knife and held it dangerously close to her neck. Sky's eyes widened, and she struggled again in fear. The tip of the knife slid down her arm, and a red line of blood appeared. She gasped and stopped struggling, and they resumed running.

Her throat began to close up as fear engulfed Sky. She used all her willpower to keep from screaming or struggling, but she couldn't stop the tears that flowed from her eyes. Were she and Randi going to be killed?

The running finally stopped when they reached some horses. Sky's captors set her down, and one began tying her hands in front of her with a vine. Sky noticed that they weren't winded or sweating, while she felt as though she had been doing the running herself. She was limp and weak. Without pause she was tossed onto the back of a horse. An Indian jumped up behind her, put his arms on either side, and grabbed the mane. She was locked against him as they took off at a gallop.

As much as she hated the arms pressed on either side of her, Sky realized that without them she would fall. She tried to grab part of the mane with her bound hands, but she couldn't get enough to steady herself. They rode on and on. The night darkened, but they didn't stop. The Indians would run the horses, slow them a while, then run again. Sky knew they had gone many miles from the camp.

How can anyone find us? she thought. *Who could they even send? Hector? He can barely walk through the campsite without mishap; he could never catch up to us. Mr. Dewell? He has to stay with the train. Colonel Stultz? No. Crane? Maybe.*

Rex Newton? He's rescued me before; maybe he'll try again. The detective? Would he put himself in danger just to take me to Hadley?

Would she die by the Indians' hands? It seemed likely. Sky swallowed the tears that choked her. Was she ready to die?

Randi said her way to heaven was already paid by Jesus. All she had to do was accept it as a gift. Was it that easy?

God in heaven, prayed Sky, *I need help! Randi needs help! I don't know you, but Randi does. Help her, please! Please, God, I don't want to die!*

Tears coursed down her cheeks as the horse raced along, carrying her away from safety. *Will you help me, God?*

God, if these Indians kill me, I don't know if I'll go to heaven. I don't know what I have to do to make you let me in! In the next second, another thought startled her. Randi said she didn't have to do anything to become a child of God but believe. *Believe what?* Her thoughts were in such a turmoil that she couldn't straighten them out to think clearly. *God, I need Randi to help me understand! Please let me live long enough to understand!*

The Indians drew up their horses and talked together with much gesturing. Sky was finally able to see how Randi was. She was sure Randi had endured the night's ride better than she had.

But Sky was shocked to see Randi lying on the horse's neck. She looked as though she couldn't raise her head.

Sky risked speaking. "Randi," she said, trembling, "are you all right?"

There was no answer. The Indians finished their discussion and took off again. Sky was abhorred when she realized that the two who had Randi were riding away from her. The other two who had Sky rode swiftly in a different direction.

She almost cried out again but stopped herself. *Oh God! Help Randi! Help me!*

They rode on and on. Sky was barely conscious when they finally stopped.

Sky struggled to open her eyes. She could feel the sun's heat baking her skin, and a raging thirst burned her tender throat. She felt eyes upon her.

Slowly her eyelids lifted. She saw the bare feet of the Indian near her. He was watching her. She turned her head slightly and found where the other Indian sat. He also was watching her.

Pain! Every movement brought fresh, raw pain. Slowly she lifted herself to a sitting position then, pushing with her swollen, bound hands, she got to her knees. The Indians watched her, expressionless.

Sweat beaded her forehead and upper lip as she placed one foot under herself and then pushed and lifted until she stood, swaying, before them. Her vision clouded, and the blackness started creeping in, but she willed it away. Still, they watched her.

The Indian standing before her reached in his belt and took out a wicked-looking knife. He flipped it in the air once, grasped it firmly, and started for her.

Sky couldn't move. She watched in helpless fear as he stepped toward her. He flashed the knife in a hypnotizing swirl before her eyes, then in a swift movement he sliced it through the vines binding her hands.

Sky drew in a ragged breath that tore at her throat. The Indians' laughter rang out in the stillness, and they pointed at her and laughed again when a shudder engulfed her as her hands began to tingle back to life. The agony nearly caused her to drop again to her knees.

The nearer man grabbed her long braid. He fingered it up and down and followed it up to her hair line. He said something to his companion, and they both laughed again. Sky's stomach turned. Then he pushed her forward, nearly causing her to fall, and pointed to two dead rabbits on the ground. He threw his knife down beside them and pointed again.

Sky understood and started for them, but he pushed her with his foot on her back so that she fell forward, hitting her shoulder on a rock. They laughed again, and the man started for her, but she hastily pulled herself to her hands and knees and crawled to where the rabbits lay. Her shoulder throbbed, and her hands cried out in pain as she tried to grasp the knife. It fell from her swollen fingers, and she bent to pick it up again.

The Indian shouted in anger at her. The one who had been seated jumped up and kicked her on her side. She groaned as she rolled with the kick; then the Indian planted his knee on her chest and held her. He sneered at her as he slapped her face. Sky's head flopped limply to the side.

She felt the darkness start to close in on her again. *Lord God, I need help!* her mind screamed.

A shot rang out! The Indian grabbed his chest and fell forward on top of her. She tried to scream, but she couldn't breathe. She couldn't breathe!

Sky struggled again to open her eyes. This time someone was speaking her name tenderly. How comforting it sounded! She felt her head lifted, and cool water ran into her mouth. She swallowed, greedy for more. Then she felt a hand smooth her hair, and she jerked away from its touch. She screamed and screamed again.

"Sky! Miss Hoffman! It's okay. You're safe! You're okay now. Settle down."

She stared in wide-eyed terror at the man in front of her while she crouched like a helpless animal before a hunter.

"Sky! It's okay! See? It's me, and there's Hector."

Sky followed his outstretched arm and saw another man. He looked familiar, and so did this one.

"Hector? Rex?" She reached an arm out to them, and her eyes saw the blood on it. She looked down at herself and saw that she was covered with blood, the Indian's blood, and she began to sob.

Rex reached her first and held her close as the sobs shook her. He rocked her gently and stroked her back, but he didn't touch her hair again.

Sky was quieting. Rex hated to upset her again, but they had to question her.

"Sky?"

He continued to hold her tightly until he felt her start to pull back. Then gently he loosened his hold but did not let her go.

"Sky, what can you tell us about Randi?"

Sky shuddered again. Hector knelt down in front of her; his face was tight, and pain filled his voice as he asked, "Sky, where is she? We've got to find her."

Fresh fear filled Sky again. *Randi!*

"They separated from us...somewhere back on the trail." Her voice was hoarse. "I...I don't know how far back; I passed out. Two Indians had her. I saw her only once. She...she didn't respond when I called her."

Sky gripped Rex's arms. "We've got to find her! We've got to help her!"

"We will, Sky!" Rex soothed her again.

Sky's eyelids dropped again as she went limp in Rex's arms.

"She's exhausted," said Rex. He gently lowered her to the ground. "Hank, you can't go alone!"

Sky's eyes fluttered, but she couldn't open them. They were so heavy! *Who is Hank?* she wondered.

"Russ, I've got to! Night will fall in a few more hours, and you know how hard it was to track Sky. We lost the others somewhere back on the trail. I have to hurry!"

"Help me get Sky back to the camp, and I'll go with you."

"You can take care of her alone, Russ. You won't need me. And one of us needs to be at the camp. There could be trouble there already. But don't you see? I've got to find Randi! She's—I've got to!"

"I understand, Hank. I'll be praying for you."

Praying. That reminded Sky. She didn't understand this mix-up of names; she didn't know who Hank and Russ were, but she had to speak to Hector. She moaned as she tried to sit up. Her shoulder!

"Hector?"

Hector rushed to Sky. Somewhere deep in her mind, Sky wondered why he didn't trip or stumble.

"What is it, Sky?"

Sky reached for his arm.

"Hector, you have to find her! I need Randi back. I need her to help me...find my way...to God."

Hector's eyes gladdened as he gently laid her down again. Her eyes were already closed.

When she awoke again, Sky smelled a campfire burning and coffee brewing. She once again made the effort of sitting up, but pain struck her body, and her shoulder throbbed with it.

Rex looked up from where he worked over the fire. Quickly he set down the stick he had been poking into the flames and hastened to her side.

"Take it easy. Go slowly, Sky." He helped settle her against a rock.

This time Sky was aware of him as his arms supported her. She felt herself flush. Sky knew little of men. She had little contact with them in her growing up years. Her boarding schools, naturally, were all female, and even though her mother and the baron went out to parties, Sky wasn't included.

Sky never thought much of it before, but lately she wondered if her mother wanted to keep her away from men and keep her as a companion. After all, she was a lonely woman living with a man she did not love. No wonder she wanted to keep her daughter close, keep her sheltered from the world of men. Sky wondered what her mother would think now of her daughter alone in a man's arms in the middle of the wilderness. Alone with the man who had never really left her mind since she first met him. Her hand went to her face, and she felt a puffiness on her cheek. *I must look awful!* she thought.

"You got hit pretty hard," commented Rex, pointing to her cheek. "I've been placing a cool cloth on it, but it still swelled up. I've also been heating some water that you can wash with if you feel able. And I've got a clean shirt in my saddlebags that you're welcome to if you don't mind the wrinkles." He smiled.

Sky looked down at her bloody shirtwaist. "Yes, please. That would be wonderful."

She watched as Rex went for the shirt and then the wash water. He handed her his bandanna to wash with; then he started to leave.

"Where are you going?" Sky felt panicky.

He turned back immediately and knelt by her side.

"I'll be here." He assured her. "I'm just going to check the area and give you some privacy. All you have to do is call; I'll hear you." He held her eyes until he saw the fear leave them. Then he rose and walked away.

Sky looked around her. She saw no one, yet she didn't feel alone. *Thank you, Lord God, for bringing Rex and Hector to rescue me. Please help Hector find Randi.*

I wonder if God can hear me talking to him? she thought. *Maybe my being rescued is because Randi is praying to God for me.*

She began unbuttoning her shirtwaist. Her left arm with the sore shoulder wouldn't cooperate. Her fingers felt numb, and her shoulder cried out in pain when she moved it. She fumbled the buttons open with her right hand and tugged and pulled until she had eased it off. Her undergarments were dirty, but the blood hadn't reached them. She was thankful for that.

She dipped the bandanna in the warm water and sponged away the dirt and blood covering her neck and shoulders. After she'd cleansed all that her right hand could reach, she put the cloth in her left hand and feebly washed her right arm.

She didn't think the arm was broken. There was movement, but the pain was intense. Finally she pulled on Rex's shirt, first over her tender left arm, then, because it was large enough, she was able to bend her right arm into its sleeve and pull it on. But the exertion cost her, and the blackness crept back over her again.

Rex called to her a few moments later but got no response. Worried, he rushed back and found her collapsed by the bloody shirt. In great panic he reached for her and checked her breathing. He noticed the red, black, and purple swelling on her shoulder and touched it gently. She groaned but didn't waken.

Anger shook Rex's fingers as he buttoned the shirt over her undergarments. Anger at the men who had done this to her. He fashioned a sling for her from a portion of his bedroll and eased it around her. The arm would be okay, but it would hurt less if it wasn't moved.

He sat back and looked at her a moment longer while he tried to steady his emotions. He had to acknowledge what he was feeling was not just anger toward her captors but a raw, savage need to protect her. *How has she come to mean so much to me, Lord, and in so short a time?* He heard what she asked Hector and knew she didn't know the LORD yet. *But she's searching for you, Father. If you can use me to help her, I'm willing.*

He had to get her back as soon as he could. She needed rest and the care the womenfolk could give her. He put the cool cloth on her cheek again, and she slowly woke up.

"I'm sorry. I keep doing that," murmured Sky. She lay still while he removed the cloth. She started to move then noticed the sling holding her arm.

"That feels better. The pain in my shoulder isn't so great." She smiled a crooked smile with her puffed cheek. "My, I must look a sight!" Her hand fumbled with her hair then smoothed down the shirt. She felt the buttons and looked down. Her face reddened, but she calmly said, "Thank you, Mr. Newton."

Rex smiled. "You're welcome, Miss Hoffman. It was my pleasure...I mean—" he cleared his throat, and his own face reddened. "I want you to try to eat something, and then if you think you can handle it we need to get you back."

"Yes. I feel better able to do that now. And I want to get back as soon as possible so you can help find Randi."

They started about half an hour later. The Indians' horses had run off, so Rex lifted Sky into his saddle before he swung up behind her. He reached for the reins, and they were off.

Sky tried to sit straight, but her exhausted body kept slumping against Rex. He didn't want to embarrass her, but finally he encircled her with one arm and pulled her against him. She resisted.

"Rest, Sky. You need it. I just want to make sure you don't fall off."

She relaxed and let him cradle her. How much more comfortable than her ride with the Indian!

"You're very sweet, Russ," she murmured sleepily.

His eyebrows shot up at the name, and he started to speak, but she was asleep.

Chapter 19

Sand Creek

Evan slowed his horse so he could think. He had been to town twice this week already; usually he went once every two weeks. He had to admit the reason: he wanted to see Ella again.

He pictured her in his mind. The beautiful blonde hair, those blue eyes. Her smile. Her laugh.

He drew up his horse sharply. What was he doing? He was as good as engaged to another woman, and here he was dreaming of Ella! But he couldn't help himself. Ella was here. He could see her, talk to her. The other woman was nameless, faceless.

But it wasn't only that. He felt drawn to Ella because of who she was, and he knew he was falling in love with her. He didn't know how it had happened or exactly when. Each short visit brought them closer; each look that passed between them spoke more than the words neither of them felt they had the right to say.

Evan prodded his horse forward again as he thought about that. He wanted Ella, not some woman he'd never met to be his wife. He wasn't sure what was the right or the wrong in his thinking, but he knew one thing. He'd tell her so today!

Arriving at the doctor's home, Evan swung down from his horse and absently noted the presence of another horse—an occurrence not unusual at the doctor's. As he let his eyes wander over the small town, he smiled in satisfaction at what he saw. Sand Creek was a good town, and Ella would be happy here. He strode purposefully up the walk, intent on his mission; he was so intent, in fact, that it caught him by surprise to find the doctor's wife waiting to greet him at the door.

"I might as well leave this door open." She laughed. "It would save me from coming to open it for all you gentlemen. How are you, Evan? If you'll just wait here a few moments, Miss Burkett is with a gentleman caller now."

Evan was surprised and looked questioningly at the woman.

"Oh, it won't take long. None of them do." She turned as Ella came to the door with a man behind her. "There, she's done with this one already," she spoke quietly to Evan.

Ella was pleased to see Evan, but before greeting him, she turned to the man behind her and held out her hand.

"Thank you for coming, Mr. Bensen. I had a pleasurable visit."

Evan looked after the man as he left. He was a farmer in the valley ten miles from here. *What?*

"Hello, Mr. Trent. It's nice to see you again."

She sounds like she's reciting to an audience, thought Evan. He looked at the two women as he shook Ella's hand.

"What's going on here?"

Florrie and Ella looked at each other and started laughing. Ella sat down with a sigh. She was tired.

"This poor girl has been receiving callers every day since you last saw her, Evan. She's plumb worn out!"

"Callers?"

"How many proposals of marriage have you had so far, dearie?"

Ella waved a hand at the door. "That makes fifteen. I never knew I was so attractive." She laughed wearily with Florrie.

"Fifteen? *Proposals?*" Evan was stunned.

"I know I came out here to marry Michael without knowing him well, but I can't understand these men that think I'll marry them right after we swap 'howdies.' I'm not ready to think of marriage again so soon. I feel like I've been widowed, even though I didn't get married."

She looked at Evan beseechingly. "You understand, don't you? You've been so good to me, making sure I was comfortable and happy with my job. I love working with the doctor. I just wish all these men would leave me alone!"

Florrie watched Evan's stricken face, and she slipped away, unnoticed by the two young people.

"That man is in love with our Ella," she mumbled to herself. "But what's he going to do when his bride gets here?"

Evan crouched down to look into Ella's face and spoke quietly, hesitantly. "I'm sorry you've had a rough time. I...I was hoping you'd feel like saying yes to one of those men... me."

Ella stared back at him. When he saw gladness leap into her eyes, he smiled. Then she looked away and spoke in a choked voice.

"I can't, Evan. If only things were different, I..." She looked back and held his gaze. "You are promised to another. You have no right to ask me."

"I'll get out of it. I'm not going to marry someone else when I love you!"

Her eyes gleamed at the words of love, but she reluctantly shook her head.

"It's not right, Evan. It was bad enough for me to come all the way here and find out my husband-to-be had died. It would have been so much worse to get here and find that he didn't want me or that he was already married. How would she feel? She's been traveling a long time, probably without money, probably depending on you for her survival."

Evan took her arms. "It would be wrong to marry her if I loved you. You know it would! Besides, look at all the men in this town looking for wives. She'd be okay."

"No! You can't dump her off to go through what I've gone through this last week. She may have already fallen in love with you. You wrote and sent a photograph with Colonel Stultz, you said."

Evan was exasperated. "I didn't write much, and the stupid picture probably didn't turn out! Ella, listen—"

"No, Evan. I can't believe it's right." Ella looked up into the face of the man who had come to mean so much to her. It was a good face. He was young, but he held a maturity far beyond the young men she had known. He was a man who knew how to work hard, how to be self-sacrificing. It was easy for her even now to compare him to all the men who had come calling on her and to see that he stood head and shoulders above them in her thinking. But she had to make him understand, even if that meant she would have to do some self-sacrificing too. "You told me the LORD would show me what to do. I don't think it's what you are...proposing. Have you even asked him?"

Evan's shoulders fell. "I want what's right too. No, I haven't asked the LORD," he admitted. "But I will. He will show us what to do. I'll meet this girl and, LORD willing, things will work out." He sighed.

"When will the wagon train arrive?" asked Ella soberly.

"About a month."

"I won't be here when it comes."

"You can't leave, Ella," Evan protested. "Please, don't leave."

"I don't want to be here when she comes. I think that would be best." As Evan started shaking his head, she hastened to add, "The doctor needs to perform a surgery for old Mrs. Poole. She'll need someone to stay with her while she recuperates, so that's where I'll be. Use the time to pray, Evan. Maybe this is the woman the LORD has chosen for you. You don't want to throw that away."

Evan ran fingers through his hair in frustration. "Promise me one thing."

She looked uncertainly at him.

"Don't accept any proposals from these men. Please, wait."

"I won't be getting married until I know the LORD wants me to, Evan. Good-bye."

Chapter 20

Wilderness

Rex and Sky sat by the glowing embers and finished their supper. The night had become too dark for safe riding, and Rex was reluctant to put Sky through more pain as they rode. He knew her arm was bothering her. Rex shuddered at how he and Hector had galloped blindly in the blackness after the girls.

Sky needed to rest too. She was still in shock after her experience, but she would be okay. He could see that even with all her femininity, she was tough. He wondered what she had gone through in her young life to make her so.

"How are you feeling now, Sky?"

Sky looked up at the question. "I feel so much better after sleeping the whole way, but I'm so worried about Randi. I really need Hector to get her back."

"You mean because you need her to tell you about God?"

Sky's head shot up. "How did you know that?"

"I heard you tell Ha—Hector about it."

"Did I? I don't remember some things anymore. My mind is fuzzy about everything since the Indians grabbed us."

"That's normal because of shock. With plenty of rest, you should clear up. But...about God..." Rex was hesitant. "Is there something I can help you with?"

Sky studied the face of the man across the fire from her. He had rescued her twice now, and she was sure that was partly the reason she felt drawn to him, but she also felt his interest in her in the way he cared so tenderly for her wounds and watched out for her comforts and in how he sometimes looked at her. Like he was now. It made her catch her breath, and it was hard for her to look away. She felt she could trust him with her thoughts.

"Normally I would be embarrassed to have someone like you know how ignorant I am of God, but I almost lost my life last night." Sky swallowed. "And I don't know what will happen to me if I die."

"What has Randi told you?" Rex asked gently.

"Randi says I don't have to go to church or give money or anything to go to heaven, which is good because I haven't," she admitted. "But I always thought I was good enough to go. I mean, I haven't been so bad that God would send me to hell. At least that's what I thought."

Rex reached into his saddle bag and pulled out a small book. Curiously, Sky watched as he turned the pages then listened as he read:

"For all have sinned and come short of the glory of God."

He continued, "These are God's words to us, telling us that we all fall short. None of us are good enough."

Sky nodded slowly. "And Randi says that Jesus paid for all our sins on the cross and he became alive again."

"That's right. Sin is no longer what separates us from God, and our goodness is not enough. Only Jesus Christ's goodness satisfies the Father."

Sky was silent, and Rex waited. "So what do I do? How do I know I can go to heaven? I don't want to face death again not knowing," she pleaded.

Rex smiled. "It is very simple, Sky. You believe that what Jesus Christ did for you was enough. There is no other way to heaven except through faith in him."

Slowly, understanding lit her eyes. "That's it! That's what Randi meant! What do I do now, Rex? Do I pray or something? Oh! I've already been praying, but I don't know if God heard me or not." Her words tumbled out in a rush in her excitement.

"Thank you, LORD!" Rex exclaimed. "Sky, you can pray if you want, anytime you want, but a prayer isn't what saves you. It's the faith you've placed in Christ this moment that makes you his child."

Sky couldn't help herself. She clapped her hands. "Oh, this is so wonderful! I really do want to talk to God, but I don't know how. What's the proper way?" she asked.

"Just like you are talking to me, Sky. Just tell him whatever you want. He already knows your thoughts."

Together they prayed, Sky thanking God for her salvation and beseeching him for Randi's safe return; and Rex doing the same. When they opened their eyes and looked at each other again, Sky asked Rex what he meant by the word *saves*.

"*Saved* is a Bible term for a child of God," he explained. "Here in Acts 16:31"—he again opened his Bible to show her—"it says, 'Believe on the Lᴏʀᴅ Jesus Christ and thou shalt be saved.'"

Sky chewed her lip while she digested the information. Her head was close to Rex's as she looked at the words, and her arm brushed against his. Suddenly realizing her close proximity, she slid back and looked up at him. Her eye was turning black from the swollen cheek. She attempted to smooth her hair.

"I have a comb if it would help," offered Rex.

Sky shook her head. "No, with only one arm I couldn't do much."

"Let me help." He started to rise.

"No! No, thank you, I'll be fine."

Rex heard the tremble in her voice. He sat back again.

Sky was relieved. She had already been held in this man's arms. While she was in need of the comfort and support, she was also conscious of the emotions that were beginning in her at his nearness. She dare not let them show.

Quickly she asked, "Who are Hank and Russ?"

Rex fumbled, nearly dropping the cup he was about to fill with coffee. He looked at her without replying.

Sky's brow puckered. "I seem to remember two people talking. They called each other Russ and Hank," she explained. Then she questioned, "But you and Hector were the only two around me, right?"

Rex nodded.

"Must be more of that fuzziness you told me about." She yawned. "Maybe it will come back to me."

"Time for you to get some sleep, Sky." Rex smoothed out his bedroll for her. He watched her get settled before returning to his coffee.

"Sky?" he asked softly.

"Hmm?"

"Why did you become a mail-order bride?" He'd been wanting to ask her that ever since he found her on the wagon train.

Sky turned over and looked at Rex. How could she explain all that had happened to her?

"I need to find my twin sister, whom I've never met. She was taken to Minnesota on a wagon train when she was a baby, so I'm going there to start searching for her. I meant to work for a while and earn money to look for her, but Hadley made it impossible for me to stay and work in New York. I had to leave in a hurry."

Sky scowled. "The wagon train was leaving from Leaf River. I would never have agreed to go, but one of Hadley's detectives was looking for me, the one who came into our camp the other night, and I had to get out of Leaf River fast, so I signed on with the train. Also, my money was stolen while I was there. There seemed little other option."

"What about this bride business?" asked Rex.

"That came with the deal," Sky replied tonelessly. "I didn't want to get married yet, but honestly, Mr. Newton"—she returned to using his formal name—"what else could I have done? No money, no way to travel, and detectives hunting me down to take me to that creep Hadley." She shivered.

"So you weren't looking for a husband?"

"No!"

"But you're going to get married anyway?" He continued to question her.

Sky felt a tear slip down her cheek. "Like I said, what else could I do? Yes, I've agreed to a marriage. I signed a legal contract, and I will abide by it." Sky spoke the words tiredly. "Good night, Mr. Newton."

She turned over again and let the tears flow silently. How she hated to be reminded of her situation! She remembered wondering if she would even live when the Indians had her. Well, she would! She should be thankful to be alive even if she still had to go through with this marriage.

Sky blinked away the tears as a new thought came to her. She was God's child now. Randi said that God wanted what's best for his children. She prayed that she would do what God wanted. Sky opened her heart to the LORD again.

Lord God, please help Randi tonight. Please help Hector find her. I don't know much about you yet, but please help me understand. Randi says you want what is best for me. If marrying this man I'm promised to is what you want, help me to do it. Would you also help me find my sister?

Then she drifted off to sleep.

Chapter 21

Wagon Train

Rex returned Sky to the wagon train the next day. As soon as they hailed the camp, the women took charge of Sky, and after Rex had been satisfied that she was being cared for, he spoke to the men.

"Hector is still looking for Miss Porter. I'll backtrack the trail and try to catch up to them."

The detective Conners was still there, and Rex strode purposefully to the man and stood before him, pointing a finger in his chest. "You will not take Miss Hoffman anywhere. Is that understood?"

Mr. Dewell intervened. "Mr. Conners has been staying on as guard while Hector's been gone."

"I'll stay until the two of you get back." Conners faced Rex. "Don't worry. I won't remove Miss Hoffman from this wagon train, but I will have to report her whereabouts. It's my job."

Rex was unsure, but Mr. Dewell took him aside. The older man's gruffness could not mask his concern as he gripped Rex in a handshake. "I won't let anything happen here, son. You just make sure we get Miss Porter back safely. I really appreciate your help, and I thank you for Miss Hoffman's return. The young lady has been through enough without being pestered by Conners. Do you think the Indians will attack?"

Rex shook his head. "It was a small hunting party, only four braves. I doubt we'll have any more trouble here. The two that had Miss Hoffman are dead."

The wagon master's eyebrows raised.

"But to be safe, sir, you ought to get these wagons rolling again. The farther from here the better. Don't worry," he said in response to the look in Mr. Dewell's eye, "we'll catch up once we find Miss Porter."

Rex renewed his supplies and changed horses with one from the train. He took a second fresh horse for Riley.

He wished he could see Sky again before he left, but there was no time. He mounted and rode back the way he had come.

Mr. Dewell watched him go then turned back to the camp and called, "Let's get these wagons rolling!"

Rex rode until nightfall. He was about to look for a place to rest for a few hours when he smelled a campfire.

Immediately he slipped from his horse's back and slowly crept forward, clinging to the shadows. He tied the horses and changed from his boots to moccasins. He ran silently through the forest and slowed when he could see the light flickering through the trees.

He inched toward the light without making a sound. He saw a man bending over the fire, his back to him. His eyes searched the shadows around the fire, and he spotted a woman. She was holding a child in her arms and was rocking back and forth.

Rex was disappointed. It wasn't them! He turned to go, and a twig snapped beneath his feet. He froze.

The man at the fire whirled around with gun drawn, and the woman had a rifle in her arms in an instant.

Rex didn't want to alarm them further so he called out, "Hello the fire!"

"Russ?"

Rex was startled. "Hank?"

Hector put his gun away. "Russ! Boy am I glad to see you! Did you get Sky back okay?"

Rex approached the fire. "Yeah, she's fine. She's going to be fine." He stared at the woman and the child now lying beside her.

Tears were running down the woman's cheeks, and she said, "Thank you, LORD." She smiled at Rex.

Dumbfounded, Rex kept looking between the woman and the child. "Randi? Who's—?"

Hector laughed. "We've got a lot to tell you, friend. Why don't you go get your horse, and we'll explain."

Rex tore his eyes from the child. She was a little thing, blonde hair, about five years old. He was truly puzzled.

"I've brought more supplies too," he said. "Be right back."

In minutes, Rex returned. "Hank, I mean, Hector—," he began.

"It's okay, she knows. You can call me Hank. And she knows you're Russ Newly posing as Rex Newton."

Russ raised his brows at Hank. "You sure that's wise to have told?"

Hank Riley laughed. "I didn't have to tell; she guessed. She had me figured out a long time ago." He smiled at Randi, and she returned his with a dazzling one of her own.

Russ still wasn't sure. "Just what does she know?"

"Everything. And don't worry; she won't let on."

Russ shrugged. He trusted Hank to know what he was doing. "How did you rescue her?"

Hank laughed again, and this time Randi joined him. Russ looked at the two of them in exasperation. What was so funny?

"I'm sorry, Russ. I guess this isn't a laughing matter, but I think you'll understand. I didn't rescue Randi. She escaped herself and rescued this little tyke to boot." He looked at Randi in admiration.

Randi explained, "I was raised with the Indians, Mr. Newly—"

Russ put up a hand. "Call me Russ," he said then added, "But call me Rex back at the camp."

Randi smiled. "I understand. Anyway, when Sky and I were captured, I couldn't understand what the Indians were saying; their language differed from the Indians I was used to, but I understood enough of their actions to have a pretty good idea what they were planning. I pretended to be weak and helpless so they wouldn't guard me so closely. That's why Sky said I didn't answer when she called to me."

"Randi was pretending then. But she didn't know they would be separated, or she would have let Sky know she was all right," Hank explained.

"I was so frightened for Sky when I realized we wouldn't be together! I prayed and prayed! The Indians took me to their camp and left me tied in a teepee. They were planning to make me their slave." She looked at Russ.

"I soon freed myself. My granddad taught me a lot about ropes," she said by way of explanation. "I crept through the camp looking for some food to take with me or some kind of weapon, and I spotted this blonde head. I knew the Indians often kidnapped white children and raised them as their own or made them slaves. I couldn't leave her there, so I picked her up and left."

Russ stared in amazement at Randi.

She continued, "I left tracks so that when the Indians realized we were gone they'd search in a different direction than what we really took. Then I picked up Becky here and carried her on my back. She was wonderful! She seemed to trust me immediately." Randi smiled down at the sleeping child. "It will be pretty hard to follow my trail after that. I kept to the rocks and streams mostly. That's another thing my granddad taught me." She grinned. "Then we met Hank comin'."

Hank and Randi looked at each other, and Randi blushed, remembering the exuberant hug she'd given him when she saw him. Russ looked from one to the other with interest before commenting.

"You must have had some granddad! But regardless of where you led the Indians, they will eventually track you back to the wagon train and—"

"Maybe not," interrupted Hank. "They think Randi is pretty helpless, so they may believe she headed in the wrong direction."

"Yes, but—"

"And they also know the wagon train will be better prepared and better guarded if they try anything there."

"I know, but—"

"And they think the other two will be bringing in Sky, so that might delay their search."

"Will you shut up, Hank!" Russ stopped his friend.

Both Hank and Randi gaped at Russ in surprise.

"What's—?"

"Listen!" Russ rubbed his hand through his hair in agitation. "They know Randi took Becky. They won't let her get away with that. Indians aren't stupid, and it won't take them long to figure out that if Randi can get untied and sneak out of their camp with another of their prisoners without any of them being aware of it, then she must know what she's doing and where she's going. They'll want revenge."

The words hung in the air as Randi and Hank stared at Russ.

"Do you think—?"

"I think they're headed in this direction right now, and if I could smell your campfire, chances are they can too."

A moment passed. Then Hank leaped to his feet and doused the fire. He spoke as he gathered his gear. "I was hoping to give the girls and the horse a rest before going on. Guess I let my guard down too quickly. Sorry, friend."

Russ met his look. "I've got a fresh mount for you, and my horse is still in pretty good shape. We'll put the gear, there isn't much, on the one here. You and Randi ride together, and I'll take Becky." He put a hand on Hank's arm. "We'll keep them safe, LORD willing."

They were packed and on the trail in minutes. Russ held a still-sleeping Becky in front of him on the saddle, and he hoped and prayed she wouldn't wake and scream at the sight of him, a stranger. He looked back at Hank and Randi and smiled to himself as he saw Randi holding herself erect in the saddle as Sky had done. Hank would coax her to relax, he was sure.

The remainder of the night passed without incident. They rode into the new campsite just as the train was readying to roll.

Russ looked for Sky, and his heart leapt when he saw her eyes gladden at the sight of him. She still wore the sling, and the bruises on her face were a riot of color, but she was beautiful.

Sky ran to the horses. "Randi! Randi, are you all right?"

Randi wakened in Hank's arms, and, realizing where they were and how she was being held, her face flamed. But the sight of Sky running toward her caused all other thoughts to flee, and she slid from the horse.

The two women embraced each other, both talking at once. The entire camp gathered around them, and for the moment Russ and Hank were forgotten. The two men looked at each other. Years of friendship enabled Russ to rightly interpret Hank's look. He was head-over-heels in love with Randi. Russ sighed. Is that what he was feeling for Sky? Did she feel anything for him? He looked at her again.

Sky caught the look in Russ's eyes, and their gaze held. She read the question there and responded with happiness that bubbled into a glorious smile on her lips. Then her look clouded as thoughts of her contract and husband-to-be entered her mind. She dropped her eyes.

Russ felt a coldness cover his heart. She felt gratitude for the rescue; that was all. What did he expect? She was planning to marry someone else anyway. He brought his attention back to Randi, who was reaching for the little girl still held slumped against him.

"Becky, we're safe now! Come, meet Sky!"

The child willingly went into Randi's outstretched arms. She looked shyly at Sky and reached out a small hand to touch her blonde hair.

"Pretty, like Mama's hair."

Randi looked surprised. "That's the first she's spoken since she told me her name," she said softly.

The others crowded in with questions and exclamations. Becky looked in awe around her until she spotted Angelina. Instantly the child began to squirm, and she struggled to get out of Randi's hold on her.

"Mama! Mama! I missed you!"

She wriggled free of Randi and ran to Angelina.

Astounded, Angelina scooped up the excited child into her arms and let herself be hugged over and over. She looked over the little, blonde head at the others and asked, "Who—? What—?"

"You must remind her of her mother," said Martha, stroking the small head. "She's been through so much; why don't we let her stay with us for now? Do you mind, Randi?"

"No, that would be great. She needs to feel secure."

The women took the little girl with them back to their wagon.

"What are the chances those Indians will come after her, Mr. Newton?" Mr. Dewell spoke to Russ.

Russ and Hank worked on unsaddling their horses while they talked with the wagon master.

"We need to stay alert. I don't know what they'll do; who does? They may come in full force and try to kill every one of us, or they may shrug their shoulders and forget the whole thing. But regardless, let's keep these wagons moving and double the guard."

"*Double* the guard? Mister, there's only you and me, Riley here, Crane, and Colonel Stultz. Conners wants to leave."

"Then we better get to where there are people to help us if they do attack."

The wagons got under way shortly after. The men were armed and watchful, though Russ and Hank were exhausted from lack of sleep.

Sky and Randi both rode so that they could talk. Their relief at being back was enormous. They talked about their salvation from the Indians as well as Sky's salvation from sin and hell.

"When you explained to Angelina how easy it was to accept the LORD, I didn't believe you. That was too simple! Then when I was faced with death and didn't know if I would go to heaven, I knew I needed God in my life. I was thankful Rex could explain again how easy it was to believe on Jesus Christ. God really helped us, didn't he, Randi!"

Randi smiled at her new sister in Christ. "He did. But you need to understand that just because you're a Christian now doesn't mean everything is going to be perfect."

"What do you mean?"

"Well, we live in a sin-cursed, evil world. Bad things are going to happen to us just like they do to unbelievers. The difference for us is that we know God will go through every situation with us, and we can rely on the verse in Romans that says 'And we know that all things work together for good to them that love God, to them who are the called according to his purpose.'"

"I have so much to learn, Randi." Sky was excited. "So even though the Indians taking us was bad, there was good that came out of it because I became God's child!"

"And maybe there were other reasons for it all to happen."

Sky looked puzzled.

"Maybe it was so we could rescue little Becky. Maybe it was so you could see your need of Jesus Christ. Maybe it was so the detective wouldn't take you away. Maybe...

maybe it was so I would fall in love with Hank." She ended quietly.

"Who's Hank? You mean, Hector? Are you really in love with Hector Riley?"

Randi nodded. She looked sideways at Sky. "He told me I could call him Hank, but I better stick to Hector."

"Hank." Sky was deep in thought. "When I was waking up, I was so dizzy and everything was fuzzy, but I thought I heard the names Hank and...and...Russ." She remembered! "So Hank was Hector. Is Russ, Rex Newton?"

Randi looked uncomfortable. "Sky, I promised not to tell. I'm sorry."

"You didn't tell, I guessed. I don't suppose you can tell me why they use different names?" She looked intently at Randi. "Please, Randi!"

"I can't, Sky! But they're both good men. There's nothing to worry about." She fell silent.

Sky was also quiet, deep in her thoughts. Then she asked, "Tell me one thing."

Randi looked uneasy. "Sky—"

"Just answer one question, please. Were these the two men I heard talking outside of camp?"

Randi sighed. "Yes. I guess you can know that. Hank said he had no idea you were nearby."

Sky nodded. Thoughts jumbled in her brain, but she could make no sense of them. What were these two up to? A new thought struck her.

"So Hector, I mean, Hank, really isn't clumsy, is he? He just puts on an act. I remember...I think...that he was quiet and he...that he moved fast out in the woods. Those were his footprints by our rock, weren't they?" She looked at Randi thoughtfully, studying her friend's flushed cheeks and shining brown eyes. "You're in love with him?"

Randi held her head in her hands. "Sky, what am I going to do? I'm promised to that creep in the photograph! I can't break my word. But Sky, it would be so wrong to marry him when I love someone else." Tears choked her words.

Sky's arm went around her friend. And Rex...Russ? Did she love him? Sky examined her feelings. She felt happy with him. She remembered his arms around her, and a blush swept over her cheeks. She was attracted to him. If she had to choose, she would definitely pick him over the blurred photograph. But did she love him?

She sighed. "Randi, does Hank love you too?"

"I think so," was the quiet reply. "Sky, if he asked me to, I'd run away from this train and that stupid contract!" Randi's breathing slowed, and she continued in despair. "But I can't, can I? I gave my word. Granddad taught me to honor my word. Sky, what can I do?"

"We can pray."

Randi's head shot up, and she looked in surprise at her friend. She wiped her eyes. "I'm sorry. You're right. Here you are a new Christian reminding an old-timer like me that God is in control. Yes, let's pray."

Chapter 22

Wilderness

"We should catch up to them by tonight. Conners must already be there, since we haven't heard from him yet." The detective wiped his brow with a handkerchief. He was sorry he had taken on this job despite the money he was making.

Rudolph Hadley stepped into the dusty black carriage, and his man, Smythe, entered after him. "Let's get going, then, Mr. Stevens."

Stevens sighed and directed his men forward. They had been on the trail of the wagon train for weeks. Hadley and his man rode in the swift carriage or on horseback, and they changed to fresh horses at every small town or settlement that was willing to trade or sell.

They made good time. It wasn't too difficult to catch up to the slow-moving wagon train. Stevens wondered if the girl would even be with it if they did. Lately he'd also been wondering why Hadley wanted her. It was his job as a detective to find missing people or investigate them, and he usually did his job without asking the reasons why as long as he got paid. Hadley was paying good money to find Miss Hoffman, but he'd never said why he wanted her. Stevens shrugged. He'd just find her. That's all he had to do.

Rudolph Hadley swayed with the moving carriage and looked out at the vast countryside.

"Primitive, isn't it, Smythe? I should think our Miss Hoffman will be glad to return to the lush, green English countryside."

"Yes, sir, I know I shall, but how will we convince the young lady to agree?" Smythe's evil eyes smiled at his employer.

"Why, she'll have no choice, will she?" Hadley's handsome face returned the smile. "These papers you forged will convince anyone that I have legal claim to her. The information I've obtained regarding her late stepfather, the baron, provided me with the idea. Thanks to your skill, we now have a marriage agreement, signed and witnessed, declaring that the baron gave his stepdaughter, Sky Hoffman, to be my wife. Of course, she'll be my fourth wife, but she need not know that."

"She may still be unwilling," remarked Smythe.

Hadley's eyes glowed with evil intent. "Yes, but she'll have no voice in the matter now, and she'll pay for spurning me. Let me see that information we got from her aunt Elaine Doane.

He flipped open a book and looked through several pages. "The mother gave birth to twins. Mrs. Doane wasn't too clear about the reasons for the other one to be sent away, was she? Sounded to me like she had something to do with it."

Hadley perused the paper again. "Sky's looking for her twin sister. Imagine two Sky Hoffmans! Now we know why she's headed north, and that's why I believe she's on this wagon train." Hadley stared out the window.

"Of course, only Sky's name would be on her stepuncle's will, but I wouldn't put it past her to share her wealth with her newfound sibling. We may have to get to her first and keep Sky from finding her."

Sand Creek

The town of Sand Creek was quiet for the night. Doors were shut, lamps blown out, and everyone was asleep.

Almost everyone. Two men stood by the blacksmith shop, talking in low tones.

"How far from here do you suppose the wagons are?"

"I think they're due here in about three weeks, if they haven't had too many delays."

The first man, the shorter of the two, was wearing a beat-up Confederate cap. He chuckled. "They're about to have a delay. Or should we call it a detour?"

The tall man sneered in answer. "Call it what you want. I'm ready to ride."

"You seem mighty anxious. You can't wait to see your 'bride,' can you? Do you know which one will be yours?"

"No. Don't matter. I'll take any I please."

The smaller man rubbed his hands together. "It's a good thing you were able to get here in time to be part of the group that ordered brides. I just hope that colonel fella didn't just run with the money. He better be out there."

"He'll be there. I put a scare into him to be sure he would. Besides, he'll want to collect on the rest of the money. Too bad he won't get the chance."

"Well, let's ride then. We'll meet up with the others halfway. They're bringing the horses. I guess it won't hurt the ladies to do a little riding, will it? At least we can move them quickly that way until we join with the railroad."

"I'm ready."

They strode to the corral and looped their horses. They mounted, and the tall man looked back at the small town.

"Nice place. Too bad they'll never see it."

Then they turned and rode into the darkness.

Chapter 23

Wagon Train

The wagons formed a tight circle for the night. Russ and Hank were sleeping at last while the other men guarded. They would be awakened if and when needed.

It was Russ's idea to arm the women as well.

"If an attack comes, they can be of great help to us. Besides, most of them are probably good shots."

When Mr. Dewell called the group together and explained the situation, Sky was amazed at the women's reactions. Most of them went to their wagons and returned with either a rifle or pistol. Even Janet came back with a shotgun.

These women think of their Bibles and guns as staples of their livelihood, marveled Sky.

Sky had never shot a gun, but she listened closely as Randi instructed her. Randi had several guns—her own as well as her grandfather's.

"You just point and squeeze the trigger. It's not hard. Is your shoulder better? Can you move your left arm yet?"

"It's not as sore now, but it sure is colorful! I think I can handle a small gun like this." She picked up a pistol. "Are we really going to shoot these people?" She shuddered.

"If we don't, they'll kill us. We'll have no choice." Randi studied Sky. "I know. I don't like it either."

Everyone was tense at the evening meal. The men ate in shifts, and the women kept close to their wagons as instructed by Mr. Dewell. They were to stay out of the open areas. Like the wick of a lamp being lowered, the evening sky darkened gradually until there was barely enough light left to make out the shapes of the wagons and trees around them. No one undressed for sleep; they just lay down, ready to spring up should the need arise. Sky could not imagine being able to fall asleep, but she followed Randi's cue and closed her eyes and before long fell into a dreamless sleep.

The attack was sudden.

War whoops and shrill screams filled the air. Arrows whistled into the small circle along with the whine of bullets and the thud or ping as each found a target.

The camp came alive with action.

The women either fired off shots alongside the men or crouched nearby to reload weapons. Sky wondered if she had truly awakened or if this was a very real nightmare as she knelt beside Randi and reloaded for her as she had been instructed. When there was a lull in the shooting, Sky looked around and gasped when two figures ran to them.

Hank's hand touched her arm; then he moved to Randi's side. He spoke in low tones to her while they waited for the next move from the Indians. Sky felt Russ's presence beside her.

"How are you doing?" he asked in a whisper.

Her sky-blue eyes turned to his, and a small smile trembled on her lips.

"I'm not nearly as brave as I'd like to be. Not like Randi."

"You're doing fine," Russ assured her. He reached for her hand and gently squeezed it while his eyes watched the surrounding shadows, his gun ready at his side.

His hand felt warm and comforting. Sky's small fingers turned and clasped his. He darted a quick look at her, and before he turned back to his surveillance, she saw the fire that brightened in his eyes. Her heart pounded, and she was sure he could hear it or feel the pulse of it. His fingers tightened.

"Sky, I—"

A volley of shots peppered the night, drowning his words. Both hands went to his guns, and Sky began reloading the weapons thrust at her.

This attack was stronger than the first attempt. Sky had no idea how long it went on. She kept loading the guns for those near her and praying with all her might for it to end.

A scream caused both she and Russ to turn. Belle was standing near her wagon, one hand on her mouth, the other pointing at an Indian with a raised knife running toward Mr. Dewell. Russ fired a shot and immediately turned and fired two more at others who had started to run into the circle.

A brightly painted brave jumped from behind the wagon at him, and Russ flipped his now empty gun in his hand and used it like a club on the Indian's neck. The man fell but was replaced by another who flashed a knife at Russ's stomach. Russ jumped back, avoiding the blade, and grabbed his own knife from his belt. The two faced each other and began to circle and feint with their weapons.

The noise of the fighting faded in Sky's ears as she watched, mesmerized by the drama before her. Fear for Russ froze her body, and all she could do was watch the hypnotizing flash of the knife blades.

The Indian was enjoying the match. He took the offense and slashed his knife, narrowly missing Russ's chest. Russ spun on his toes and struck out with his knife, but the Indian rolled away from him.

Sky came to herself with a jolt when the knife suddenly drew blood from Russ's arm. With animal instinct, she reacted. The small pistol was in her hands, and she fired as the Indian dove at Russ's heart in a deadly move.

The Indian's side burst into a flame of red, and he lifted on his toes then fell into the dirt. Russ swung to look at her white face and trembling hands. His breath came in gasps as he knelt and took her in his arms. She pulled him close for an instant; then they drew apart, and Russ picked up the pistol and turned back to the fighting.

With shaking hands, Sky continued to reload the weapons.

I love him!

Astonished by her thoughts, Sky became very aware of Russ beside her. It didn't matter that they were in the midst of an attack with bullets and arrows all around them. For a brief, unforgettable moment in time she rejoiced in loving this man.

The attack continued, and the people in the little circle were weakening. Sky saw Crane take a bullet in his arm. Arrows appeared everywhere, whizzing through the darkened sky as the night turned to an inky black, slashing into the canvas on the wagons. Then a new sound of shooting erupted from outside the camp!

The tired defenders looked at one another in fear. A new tribe? More to fight? Would they be able to hold out?

Then Hank called out, "They're helping us! They're shooting at the Indians!"

The group's spirits rose, and they renewed the fight in earnest. The Indians fell back under the fresh onslaught, and eventually the evening quieted.

"Hello the camp!" called out a voice.

"Welcome!" answered Mr. Dewell.

The people of the wagon train kept their posts as they watched men entering their circle.

Three men walked in, leading horses, and a black carriage followed. One man stepped up to Mr. Dewell, but he was barely visible in the fading light.

"Looks like you folks were having some trouble here." He took the hand Mr. Dewell offered, and they shook.

"You came at the right time, stranger. We're grateful for the help."

Sky was watching the meeting along with the others when she noticed Russ and Hank exchange looks. They seemed uneasy about the new people and kept their guns at the ready.

Conners left his post and walked over to the man. "Mr. Stevens! What are you doing way out here, sir? I was about to send my report back to you."

Russ and Hank looked as perplexed as the others, and Hank shook his head at Russ as they lowered their guns.

Sky felt a sinking sensation in her stomach. It couldn't be!

The man named Stevens walked over to the carriage and opened the door.

"Everything all right in here, sir?" he asked.

"Never better!" came the reply. "That was quite exhilarating, Stevens. I had hoped for some action on your western frontier, and I got it. Now let's see what we've found here."

As the moon found an opening in a cloud and shone down on the small group, a polished black boot appeared, and a tall, handsome man stepped out and looked around him. He thrust out a hand to Mr. Dewell and announced, "Rudolph Hadley here. Are you the man responsible for absconding with my betrothed, Miss Sky Hoffman?"

Chapter 24

Wagon Train

"What do you mean 'betrothed'?"

A tight-lipped Sky sat facing a smiling Rudolph Hadley. Randi stood beside her, one hand on her shoulder, her protective stance evidence of her distrust of the newcomers. The men were still standing guard. Sky wished Russ was closer. She disliked even being near Hadley; he made her feel uneasy.

"My dear, I tried to explain on the ship and again in New York, but you left without my knowledge. Your stepfather and I had an agreement. It's all right here." He waved to some papers before him. "He gave your hand to me before he died. Everything is legal; see for yourself." White teeth flashed into a smile.

"You're lying! You never even heard of me or my stepfather before. My mother would have known if there had been an agreement, and she would have prevented it." Sky sincerely hoped she was right, but doubt was creeping into her mind. Could the baron really have done something like this? He had no love for her, and he might have made an agreement just to get rid of her. She recalled him saying something about "arrangements." Funny how all that had been forgotten in the chaos after his death. Her head ached, and her shoulder started throbbing again after all she'd just been through.

"I will never marry you! Leave here! Leave me alone!" She rose and took Randi's arm. Without looking at Hadley again, she walked away.

"I won't be easy to be rid of, Sky. I have legal claim to you. There's nothing you can do about it."

Sky kept walking, and Randi watched her closely. Sky's face was white and shock glazed in her eyes. Russ appeared by their side and questioned Randi over Sky's head, but Randi only looked at him helplessly.

"Sky? Are you okay?" Russ gently stopped her. "What does Hadley want? Why did he follow you here?" As yet, Hadley didn't know Russ was with the train.

Sky stared blankly at Russ, seeming to look right through him. She murmured, "It can't be true! The baron didn't hate me that much, did he?" Tears rolled from her eyes.

"Shhh! It will be all right." Russ pulled her to him. *Baron?* Randi stood quietly watching as he continued, "I won't let anything happen to you."

The strong arms soothed Sky, but she came to herself and pulled away.

"What am I going to do now? He says I have to marry him. He says he has legal claim to me." Her eyes searched his.

Russ appeared to make up his mind.

"He can't marry you," he said slowly and carefully, "if you're already married to someone else." He let the words sink in.

"You mean...my contract?" Sky was puzzled.

Russ cleared his throat, "Well, I—"

"Russ!"

Russ turned his head at the sharp whisper. Hank stood in the shadows, motioning to him urgently.

Russ squeezed Sky's arms and quickly said, "I have to go."

Sky and Randi stared into the dark where the two men had been.

The next morning Russ was gone.

Dark clouds rolled in with the new day. Sky scowled. They matched her mood.

It had been two weeks since Hadley and his detectives had joined them. Two weeks without a word from Russ. When she questioned Hank, he had looked apologetically at her but only shrugged his shoulders. For some reason he could tell her nothing. To make matters worse, Hank had returned to being the clumsy 'Hector' around the camp. Because of Randi, Sky said nothing. But she was tired of it, tired of everything that had to do with men.

Hadley was the worst. He sickened her. He had most of the women in the camp convinced that he was a wonderful person. Even Violet fawned all over him.

"I can't understand you, Sky Hoffman. If a rich, handsome man like that came all this way after me, I'd be in heaven! I'd be thrilled to marry a man like him."

Sky felt anger burn in her. At least the men were on her side. Mr. Dewell accepted the newcomers out of gratitude for their help with the Indians, but Sky knew he distrusted Hadley and Smythe. The detectives were decent men, just doing their jobs, but the Englishmen were up to something, he was sure.

Colonel Stultz openly disdained Hadley and made no effort to be nice to him. He wasn't about to let him take one of the brides from the train.

Of course, Hank was on guard around Hadley. Sky knew he was protective of her, and she was grateful for that, but Crane's attitude surprised her the most.

Generally Crane stayed away from the women and the camp when he wasn't on guard or scouting ahead of the train. He was surly and unpleasant. Sky thought he'd probably get along just fine with Smythe since they were two of a kind, but Crane openly disliked the men that had joined the train. He wanted them gone and made sure they knew it.

Even though Sky avoided any contact with Rudolph Hadley since the first night he arrived, she knew he was keeping his feelings hidden beneath his handsome smile. He was up to something, she was sure. She watched as he worked on winning the confidences of the women by helping them with their chores or complimenting them or sharing delicacies from his own supplies with them. She balled her fists in frustration. *Can't they see what a phoney he is?*

Then one day, he approached Sky with an offer. He met her and Randi by the fire as they prepared the day's meal. Randi bristled as he came near, but Sky just kept working as though he didn't exist.

"My dear Sky, I know you dislike the thought of these new circumstances. They come as a surprise to you."

She continued peeling the wild onions Randi had found and put them into the kettle without looking up. She felt more than saw Hadley clench his teeth to keep control of his temper. His smooth voice went on.

"I have learned that you seek a twin sister here in America."

Sky's hands stilled. *Someone on the train has been talking.* She resumed her work.

"I want to help you. You will become my wife soon, and as my wife you will have everything you desire. I only want to make you happy, my dear. So I propose to send these detectives off in search of your sister for you. Will that make you happy? It will cost a great deal, but I want to prove to you that I care deeply about your happiness."

Sky looked briefly at the man. When she saw his quick smile, she regretted letting him see her interest.

"I understand that twenty years ago she traveled with a family on a wagon train. If the woman looks anything like you do, my dear, we will find her in no time. Beauty such as yours is noted and remembered wherever it goes." He tipped his hat and walked away.

Sky stared after him. Why would he bother looking for her twin for her? What did he hope to gain? She still would never marry him.

Three detectives left the next morning; Conners being one of them. That left Hadley, Smythe, their driver, and Mr. Stevens. Crane still wasn't pleased with the remaining men. In fact, he was more surly than usual. Sky thought perhaps his arm bothered him even though Belle had bandaged it and declared that it was healing fine.

Two days later they found out the reason for his behavior. The train rested for the noon meal. It was hot. Everyone was looking for a shady place to rest for a while, and a lazy feeling covered the camp.

They were not prepared for the men who rode up with guns drawn.

There were eight of them; hard cases all of them. They quickly disarmed the men in camp, including Hank, who couldn't hide his frustration at being caught unawares. All the men, that is, except Crane.

"Thought you'd never get here!" he complained. "I'm sick and tired of babysitting this bunch."

"You're not done yet, Crane. We've got to take them a long ways yet before we get paid in full. But at least now we can have a little fun with them on the way."

There were gasps and screams from the women, and Martha and Angelina held tightly to the children.

One of the men strode over to Colonel Stultz. "Remember me, colonel? I see you took my advice and didn't just run with the money. Which one of these were you planning to pair off with me?" He leered at the women who were cowering by their wagons.

Sky felt a new fear overtake her. She had feared death and conquered it, but this was fear of something worse. These men planned more harm to them than she could imagine. Then she took a sharp breath as she recognized the man's face.

He turned at the sound. His eyes swept over her, and a look of triumph flashed into them. "Looks like I got the prize, fellas!" he shouted and started for her, but Randi quickly stepped in front of Sky. She held up the photograph she had in her hand. "So you're the vermin in this picture," she said in disgust. The insolent face of the unwashed man in the photograph mirrored the unshaven, unkept outlaw before her.

Ned Bolter stopped and leered as he looked Randi up and down. "Looks like they both want me!" he crowed. "I can handle you too, darlin'!" He reached for Randi.

"Not now, Bolter!" the leader ordered. "Get over here and help tie these men. I get that fancy gent's gold watch too."

"Just what is your intent, mister?" Janet Conly demanded the man's attention, and her schoolmarm attitude was not lost on him. Most of the others turned to her as well, for her authoritative tone commanded it of them. Randi inched back to the wagon and reached under the canvas. She caught the eyes of Martha and Angelina and swung her eyes to the others, who quickly caught their meaning. In a whisper she said to Sky, "Distract them. Help Janet."

Sky was unsure. She saw the other women reach in their wagons too, and though she understood what they intended to do, she felt like she couldn't move. Some of the men were turning back again, she had no time to think, so quickly she stepped beside Janet.

"Yes, what do you men want here?"

The men swung around again to get a better look at her. The leader stepped closer to Sky.

"You'll bring a good price, won't she, boys?"

"Price? I'm not for sale, sir!" Sky's hands trembled at her sides.

"Oh yes, you are! You're going to make us rich! South of the border they pay good money for merchandise like you."

Sky's stomach turned. She'd rather be kidnapped by the Indians! Then she saw Hank nod to her to continue. He was also inching for the gun lying on the ground behind him.

Sky tried to pray for help as she continued. She swung her skirts, and her slender legs showed for an instant as she sat on a log.

The men stepped closer. She was a beauty!

Her English accent captivated them as she strove to keep their attention. "Since I've come to this country, I've been bargained for, kidnapped, contracted for marriage, and hunted down by detectives. Everyone claims to own me. I'm sick of it!" She reached for the coffee pot and poured a hot cup of coffee. The men were awed by her audacity, but still they watched her.

She pointed to Hadley. "Even he thinks, because he has so much money, that he can buy me!" The men's eyes swung to Hadley. He was sitting on the ground near Smythe; his hands were tied, his gold watch was gone, and an evil look was centered on Sky for bringing him to their attention.

The leader prodded Hadley with his foot. "Where's all this money, Dandy? You got it hidden somewhere?"

"Check his carriage. He probably has bags of it hidden under the seat." Sky looked disdainfully at Hadley. He glared back at her.

Two men ran to the carriage and began a search. Some watched them, and the others began again to turn. Hank stopped his movements. Sky searched for something to do.

She swallowed her nervousness; then she crooked a finger at the leader. "Come here," she coaxed.

He looked warily at her, and the other men watched her curiously.

"Maybe you and I can make a deal," she spoke softly, and he stepped closer.

"What kind of a deal? You aren't in a very good bargaining position, honey." He chuckled.

Sky smiled sweetly at the man. Her hand gripped the coffee cup tighter as Hank slowly started bending to his gun.

"I didn't want to go to Sand Creek anyway. And I don't want to go to Mexico either. Couldn't you just marry me yourself?"

He looked at her and smiled back. "I wish I could; I really do. We'll have to talk about that some more—."

The men in the carriage let out a whoop. "He's got money all right!" they called.

The leader turned to the noise, and Sky flung the hot coffee at him. He threw up his hands, and guns went off all at once.

Sky threw herself to the ground and crawled under the wagon beside Janet.

"Good work, Sky. You kept them busy long enough for us to get our guns." She fired her shotgun, and a man grabbed at his leg.

The men were completely surprised by the attack from the women. They didn't expect any of them to be armed, so it was over quickly.

Hank gathered the remaining men who were standing and instructed them to keep their hands up. He put Belle and Nola on guard, and Bridget and Gretchen began tying hands. Randi untied the men from the wagon train.

Hank spoke to the prisoners, and the others listened in amazement. "You men are under arrest. There will be guards coming to take you to jail until your trials."

"Riley?" Colonel Stultz stared at him.

"Hector, what do you know about this? What guards?" Mr. Dewell demanded.

"My name's Hank Riley, sir. I work for the Pinkertons."

The women looked even more surprised, the men amazed, Randi looked on in admiration, but Sky looked confused.

"What's Pinkertons?" she asked Randi.

"They're detectives, I think."

"Just what I need, more detectives." Sky sighed. "And Russ, is that what he is too?"

"I guess so," said Randi; her eyes hadn't left Hank.

Sky saw where Randi's attention was centered, and a new thought hit her. "Randi, if that man Bolter was supposed to be your husband, what happens to you now?"

"She marries *me*, I hope." Hank turned to the two women. The whole camp stopped and stared. Randi's face flamed, but she kept her eyes on Hank.

"Will you?" he asked.

"Yes," she replied in a quiet, clear voice.

"Now wait a minute," interrupted Colonel Stultz. "There is still the money—"

"It's right here." Hank stopped him and held out an envelope to the man. Randi's eyes moved to the envelope the colonel opened and the money he began counting. Then she lifted her eyes back to Hank's, and a look of love passed between them.

Sky's vision blurred and a tear slipped out of her eye. How long had he had that money ready?

Mr. Dewell cleared his throat. "Hector, I mean, Hank, you had us all fooled! What happens now? How did you know these men were coming? Why didn't you tell me?"

Hank held up his hand. "We knew the gang was working in this area. When news of this wagon train of brides was out, we knew it would be a prime target. We also knew the gang worked by getting one of their men in with the people they were planning to kidnap. We didn't know who it was, it could have been any of you, even one of the women. Turned out to be Crane."

"What would have happened to us in Mexico?" asked Angelina.

Hank looked at Angelina and spoke gently. "You would have been sold into white slavery."

Angelina's hand flew to her mouth, and she clasped Becky to her with her other hand. The others reacted in the same way.

"Thank you, Mr. Riley, for saving us from such a fate," spoke Janet sincerely.

"No need to thank me, ma'am. You all did it. I'm very proud of all of you."

"What happens now?" Mr. Dewell asked again.

"There are guards coming; I expect them by tonight. They will escort these men away. My partner, Russ Newly— you know him as Rex Newton—was sent to round up the rest of the gang that is waiting farther south." He looked at Sky. "He won't be back until the job is done. I'll stay on with the train until you get to Sand Creek; then I hope my wife and I can go back to Illinois together and hand in my resignation. I think I'll try my hand at ranching, if that's okay with you." He looked at Randi.

She nodded happily.

The women crowded around Randi and congratulated her. Sky didn't get a chance to talk to her until evening.

"Randi, I'm so happy for you! The LORD really worked everything out for you, didn't he! Just like you said." Sky hugged her friend. "I'm trying to pray like you told me, but

I'm still not very good at it. I just kept saying, 'God, help me!' the whole time the gang was watching me."

"And he did. Just talk to him like you talk to me, and he'll work things out for you too, according to his will. Keep trusting him." Randi saw the sadness creep into her eyes.

"It seems that he's not working it out for me and Russ, does it? He's far away, and I've got Hadley breathing down my neck. You'd think if God wanted Russ and me together like you and Hank, he would have him here, wouldn't you?"

Sky drew a ragged breath. "I have to make a decision in about a week. I'll have not only Hadley to deal with but also the man in this blurry picture. The only way to prevent Hadley from claiming me is to do what Russ said and marry someone else. Since I'm under contract to him"— she pointed at the photograph—"I guess I'll have to marry him."

"Russ might be back by then," Randi said thoughtfully.

"Even if he were," Sky spoke helplessly, "he never said he'd marry me. I don't even know if he loves me."

Chapter 25

Wagon Train

Hadley called Stevens over to him. "What do those men of yours have to report?"

"Well, sir, without a telegraph line here it takes time to get reports." He had a man riding to the nearest town with a line, relaying messages. "There were several trains traveling at that time. Few kept records. The people scattered all over the area, so it's like looking for a needle in a haystack."

Hadley's scowl deepened. "What about the men out here? No one has information about a woman who looks like Sky Hoffman?"

Stevens shook his head. He was tired of this job and this man, yet he remained respectful. "No one yet, sir."

"We'll be in Sand Creek soon. We'll continue looking from there. I just have to keep Miss Hoffman under a watchful eye; that will be all, Stevens."

"Yes, sir." The detective left.

Hadley contemplated his problem. He felt his "legal" papers would pass inspection and enable him to take Sky with him, but he had to be careful about forcing her. One thing he had learned about this country so far was that the people didn't take to his commanding ways. His money and position meant little to them. If he forced Sky to leave against her will, someone would try to stop him, and out here they stopped men with a rope.

Mr. Dewell approached Hadley the next day. "Mr. Hadley, I thank you again for the help you and the men gave us when we were in a spot back there, but now I'm going to ask you to move on."

Hadley looked coldly at the man.

"I've got a job to do, and that is to get these women to Sand Creek. Now I know you have business with Miss Hoffman, but it doesn't appear the lady is willing to talk to you, so you can just meet up with her again in town and finish your business there." The wagon master took a deep breath. He was tired of having the English dandy around.

Hadley squinted his eyes at the man. "As you wish, Mr. Dewell, but let me warn you. Miss Hoffman is betrothed to me. She will arrive in Sand Creek with the rest of this train, or you will be held responsible."

"Don't threaten me, mister." Mr. Dewell returned the cold, hard look of the man and left.

The train formed its final circle. The next day they would be in Sand Creek. Colonel Stultz wanted to keep moving and arrive there early—after all, he had money to collect— but the women were adamant. They wanted time to clean up and prepare themselves before they met the men.

Bridget giggled as she carried water to the fire. "Imagine! We'll be saying our 'I dos' tomorrow, and tomorrow night we'll be—Oh good evening, Mr. Dewell. Can I get you some stew?" She burst into giggles again as she turned and saw the other women's expressions. Gretchen frowned at her sister then smiled. She was going to enjoy this last evening together too.

The men made themselves scarce as the women began heating water for bathing. Randi and Sky sat apart from the others. They were quiet.

"Will you and Hank marry right away tomorrow?" asked Sky. She was already feeling lonesome. The two had formed a friendship stronger than that of blood, and Sky felt she was losing a sister.

"Hank said we probably should wait and marry when we get back to Illinois where his family lives, but we want to travel back as husband and wife, sort of a honeymoon." She blushed. "So I guess we'll marry as soon as the preacher is free. He'll be busy tomorrow. Will you stand up with me, Sky?"

"Of course, Randi. I just wish you didn't have to leave so soon."

"Hank said he wanted Russ to stand up for him, but he doesn't know when he'll see him again, and he can't wait. I mean...he has to get back."

Sky smiled absently at Randi's slip, but her mind was on Russ. Would she ever see him again? She prayed hard last night, asking God to show her what to do. She still didn't know. Mr. Dewell had finally told her that he simply could not remember the name of the family that took the baby twenty years ago, another obstacle in her future.

"I'm relieved that Hadley is gone for now, but I'm worried about seeing him in town. What will he try next?"

"You don't believe him, do you?"

"Not anymore. If the baron had made an arrangement with him, I would have heard long ago. Somehow he has gotten information about me and is using it to trap me. I just don't know why. I certainly don't have any money."

The women sat quietly for a few minutes; then Randi, in an effort to cheer Sky up, said, "Let's go visit Martha and Angelina and the kids. I want to see Becky again."

Angelina was bathing Becky in a small tub. The pretty girl was laughing and playing in the water.

"What will happen to Becky?" asked Sky quietly.

Angelina looked at the little girl with love in her eyes. "I hope she stays with me. I'm going to ask my man to take her as well as this little fellow." She patted her growing abdomen. "If he won't, he won't get me either."

Sky was about to ask about the contract, but she didn't. They were all sick of being reminded about their commitments.

Martha was putting her two to bed in the wagon for the last time. "It will be good to sleep in a house again, won't it? And to cook on a stove and sweep a floor. I'm looking forward to everything except the man behind it all." She laughed nervously. "Tomorrow we'll know if this has all been worth it." She took out her photograph and looked at it.

The girls said their good nights and strolled back to their wagon, pausing to speak to their friends as they went.

"Janet was sweet at the Bible reading, wasn't she? I feel like we've all become a family, except for Violet. I hope we can all stay in touch with one another."

"Maybe Hank and I will settle here when we're done in Illinois. Wouldn't that be great?"

"I don't know if I'll be here or not," replied Sky. "Tomorrow I'll find out."

Chapter 26

Sand Creek

Evan stood nervously on the boardwalk with the other men. They were all freshly bathed and shaved, wearing their best clothes.

We look ridiculous, thought Evan. The men shifted their feet and looked sheepishly at one another. Some of the other men in town, especially the married ones, came out to stare and snicker at the red-faced men, but mostly they were anxious to get a look at the women too.

Taylor Gray tied his horse and buggy at the rail and walked to the others with a bunch of flowers held in his hands. He was a tall, handsome man, sure of himself. Evan thought of his farm south of town. The man spent more of his money on his fancy buggy and horse than he did on his crops and home.

The barber hurried out of his shop after flipping the *closed* sign in place. He paused to comb his already neatly parted hair before joining the group.

Evan noticed two strangers watching from across the street. They had been in town a few days according to the Nolans, who saw most of what went on in the small town. It seems the tall man was asking around if anyone had seen a blonde woman about twenty years old. Evan thought of Ella out at the Widow Poole's. As far as he knew, no one had mentioned her; but then, people kept pretty much to themselves and minded their own business here.

Hoof beats pounded down the street, and Evan turned with the others to see Duke Tunelle. He frowned slightly and shook his head. The man hadn't even cleaned up for his wedding day! He still wore his overalls from working in the fields, and his long hair and beard were uncombed.

Clyde Moore, the blacksmith, stood by Evan and nervously tapped his foot. "Shouldn't they be here by now?"

The banker, Bert Davies, answered impatiently, "They'll come. Quit that tapping! You're driving me crazy!"

Evan couldn't help smiling. He didn't quite share the men's feelings, but he couldn't help being amused by them. He would meet this girl like he promised Ella, and he planned to see her settled and to explain to her that he wasn't ready to marry yet. Hopefully she'd see someone else she wanted, and he'd be free. He'd even pay the colonel the remainder of the money, and his obligation would be over.

Again he looked at the other men. Some were sitting on the bench in front of Nolan's store; others leaned up against the building. Some just stood awkwardly, looking up the road. *I guess we're all here. All except...Where's Ned*

Bolter? Evan shrugged. *He's probably getting a drink over at the saloon.*

Jasper Riggs, freshly shaved and with a scrubbed face, was the first to see the wagons. He excitedly called to the others, "There...look there. They're coming!"

The wagons finally rolled into view. All the men rose and stood, straining to see the women riding on the seats. Colonel Stultz rode ahead and descended from his horse while the wagons continued to slowly come closer.

In his usual manner, the colonel raised his arms for the men's attention. "Gentlemen, the women are here as I promised. Before they arrive, I believe some money is due me."

The audacity of the man angered Evan, but the others handed the man their money willingly and turned back to watch the wagon train approach.

Mr. Dewell called a halt to the wagons, and the women sat looking at the men on the boardwalk. No one moved as they stared at one another. Finally Janet Conly stepped from her wagon, followed by Nola. The O'Donnells joined them, Bridget clutching Gretchen's hand and holding her photograph with her other. Violet and Gertie hurried up, and Belle and Bertha timidly stepped behind them.

Angelina and Becky walked behind Martha, who held her baby in her arms and her little son by the hand. Martha took another look at her photograph then scanned the faces in front of her. Sky and Randi stood back and watched.

The men also watched as Martha approached them. The sight of two children came as a surprise. Evan swallowed nervously. What if she was looking for him? What if he had promised to marry her, and he had two kids to provide for too? But she passed by him.

Martha paused in front of Jasper Riggs. She consulted the picture again and then showed it to him as well.

"Is that you?" she asked in a shaky voice. She watched his reaction closely as he looked at her and the children. He seemed stunned, but he nodded.

"My name is Martha Scott; I am a widow and these are my children. This one's Percy"—she gently shoved the little boy forward—"and the baby's name is Peter." She swallowed nervously. "I know you've signed a contract, sir, but I want you to know that if you don't want me and the children, we will—"

"No!" Jasper held up a hand. "I...I can't believe it!"

Martha stared at the man, unsure of what he was trying to say.

"Not only do I get a wife," he said, looking admiringly at her, "but I also get a family!" He knelt down to Percy and held out his arms. The youngster looked at his mother then went to the man. Jasper picked him up and held out his hand to Martha. She smiled and took it. Mr. Dewell let out his pent-up breath, and a wave of relief swept over the group of men and women.

Belle came forward next. Timidly she looked at the big man next to Evan. "Clyde Moore?"

He nodded and stepped closer, twisting his hat brim in his hands.

"I've been looking at your photograph for a long time. I only hope you like me as much as I like you!"

His answer was to sweep her off her feet and twirl her around. "I like you just fine, ma'am."

The nervous brides and grooms laughed, and the tension eased.

Gretchen started up the steps next then looked back to a frozen Bridget. Her sister motioned for her to follow, but still the girl didn't move.

Gretchen looked embarrassed; then with a twinkle in her eye she said, "I think we finally found something that will make you stop talking."

The women laughed, and Bridget good-naturedly looked at her sister with a feigned scowl. "All right now. You've had your laugh." She turned to the men. "Where are the Nolans?"

Jonas and his younger brother, Harry, stepped forward.

"Sisters? Hey, now that's great, isn't it, Harry? Who gets whom?" He laughed as they looked at each other.

Gretchen looked at her photograph again and turned to Harry. "My name's Gretchen O'Donnell. Glad to meet you." She held out her hand. The bashful Harry took her fingertips in his own then dropped them as if he had been burned.

Bridget and Jonas looked at each other, and a huge grin spread across the man's face. "So you're the talkative one? What's your name?"

Bridget just stared at the man wide-eyed. Her mouth moved, but no words came out.

Worried, Gretchen started for her sister, but Jonas spoke again. Uncertainty was in his voice, "Won't I do, ma'am?"

That brought Bridget to herself, and she quickly replied, "Oh no, you'll do just fine! Just fine indeed!"

Nola approached a quiet man who said his name was Roy Hill, a farmer outside the town. And Bertha smiled at the barber, who beamed back at her and offered his arm.

Janet was about to speak when little Becky suddenly squirmed out of Angelina's arms and began pointing and yelling.

"Papa! Papa!" she cried, and to everyone's astonishment she ran to the heavily bearded, long-haired Duke Tunelle. The man stood like a statue, his eyes staring at the little blonde angel.

Becky reached him and threw her arms around his legs. "Papa! I missed you! Papa!"

"Rebecca? Becky?" The man shook himself out of his trance and bent to the child. He held her away from him and stared at her face. His hands felt her hair and ran over her eyes and nose. "Is that you? Are you alive? Oh God, can it be possible?" He clutched her to him, and tears streamed from his face.

The others watched in amazement. Evan couldn't believe the child could possibly recognize the man under the hair and beard. Was it really one of Tunelle's children, alive after a year of living with the Indians? Were any of the others alive? But no, he remembered the others had been found dead. It was assumed the youngest had been killed too.

A man and woman approached Tunelle and the child. Duke became aware of their presence and stood with

Becky in his arms, but he had to rub at his eyes with a shirt sleeve before he turned to them.

Hank stood with his arm around Randi's waist and introduced himself to the man. "Sir, my name is Hank Riley, and this is my bride, Miss Miranda Porter." He held out his hand and shook the man's. "Miranda and another young woman from the train were kidnapped by Indians on our journey. Fortunately they escaped without harm, and Miss Porter here also rescued your daughter."

Becky turned around to them but kept her arms firmly about her father's neck and exclaimed, "Randi, look! It's my papa!"

Duke Tunelle struggled to find words. "I...I don't know what to say. I thought they were all gone." His eyes were misted as he looked at Randi. "Thank you, miss...I just don't know how to thank you!"

Angelina watched quietly from beside the wagon with tears streaming down her face as she watched the reunion of father and daughter. This was the man in her photograph. She wondered if he would remember he was expecting a bride today or if, with all the memories of his family coming back to him, he would even want a bride.

But Becky remembered her first. "Papa! You have to see Angie; she's been taking care of me. She's just like a mama."

Duke turned and followed his daughter's pointing finger to the small form by the wagons. Angelina hesitated then wiped her eyes and walked to them.

"Angie, look! It's my papa! We prayed God would help us find him, and he did! Angie, I love you!" Becky flung her arms around Angelina, pulling her closer to Duke.

Angelina hugged the girl then gave her back to her father. Duke looked at her curiously, and she worked up the courage to speak.

"I guess I'm your bride, if you still want me. My name's Angelina—"

But Duke cut her off. "I want you. Me and Becky want you very much, Angie. I'm Duke. Duke Tunelle." He rubbed a hand over his face. "I'm sorry. I guess I need to clean up a bit."

Evan sighed with relief as he saw the ice begin to thaw from the man's heart.

But Angelina shook her head. "Mr. Tunelle, there's something else you need to know before you decide." She cast a nervous glance at the crowd around them but took a deep breath and continued anyway. Sky prayed silently for her friend.

"I'm expecting a baby, but I—" She tried to go on but found the words were too hard for her to say.

Duke held up his hand to stop her attempt. Understanding was in his eyes, and he prevented her from saying more. "I want both of you, then, Angelina. God has brought my Becky back to me and blessed me with you and a child. I am an undeserving man, not worthy of this gift. My only hope is that you will be happy with us."

She looked deep into his eyes and nodded at what she saw there. She took her place beside him.

The group now turned back to the remaining women. Evan wondered which one would approach him.

Violet had waited long enough. She had been watching the handsome man with the flowers for some time, not daring to believe her luck. He was the best-looking man there. She raised her head and stepped up to him.

"I'm Violet Boothe, and you are?"

Taylor Gray swept his eyes over the pretty girl and smiled, "Taylor Gray, at your service. These are for you."

Violet took the flowers and looked at the other women to see if they were watching. She smiled smugly.

Janet stepped forward next and looked long and hard at the remaining three men. Evan inwardly cringed as her stern face swept over his features, and he let out a pent-up sigh of relief when her gaze stopped on the man to his right.

She marched up to the man and spoke. "My name is Janet Conly, and I believe in reading and obeying the Good Book. What about you?" she demanded.

The startled man swallowed, his Adam's apple bobbing with the effort. He nodded his head up and down and mumbled, "Yep, me too."

"Well, then, what's your name? I hope it's a decent one. I don't want to be saddled with a foolish name."

The man squirmed under her sharp gaze. "George. George Spencer, ma'am."

Janet gave a quick nod. "Glad to meet you, Mr. Spencer." She planted herself beside the doubtful-looking man.

Gertie fingered her photograph and looked between Bert Davies and Evan. Once again Evan felt relief as she walked to the man beside him.

Bert Davies smiled at the attractive girl. "Hi, miss. I'm Bert Davies. I'm the banker here in Sand Creek. Welcome."

Violet's head turned at the word "banker," and she looked sharply at Bert, wondering if she should make a switch, but Taylor squeezed her hand, and she looked back at him with a smile. He was still better looking than any of them, and by the look of his clothing, he seemed well-to-do.

Gertie told Bert her name and nervously took her place beside him.

That left Evan. He and the others looked at the empty wagons, and for a moment he thought he would be rid of his problem altogether. Then Sky stepped from behind one of the wagons.

She had put on one of her best dresses for the day, and she wore her long golden hair down in a loose braid. In moments she caught everyone's attention.

Evan felt something leap inside him. He blinked his eyes and looked again. The woman was watching him closely. He had to admit she was the most beautiful woman of the group. She was as pretty as Ella.

Evan shifted his feet. Ella. He thought of the woman he believed he loved and couldn't help comparing her to this woman. They were the same size and had the same color hair, although Ella wore hers differently.

Sky walked closer to Evan, all the eyes watching her. She held out the photograph, and he tore his eyes from hers and glanced down at the blurred image. He smiled.

"I guess that's supposed to be me."

Sky couldn't help responding with a smile of her own.

Their eyes locked, and something passed between them. Evan looked away; his mind was racing. He was suddenly glad Ella wasn't here. He felt confused.

Colonel Stultz beamed at the people before him. It had worked! They all seemed happy. He wiped his brow. Was he ever glad that was over!

The couples started moving. Some began unloading wagons and reloading onto new ones. Others headed for the preacher, who had set up in the doctor's parlor to perform weddings that day.

Sky and Evan stood uncertainly watching the others. Evan wasn't sure how to begin what he wanted to say, and Sky was trying to think how to tell him she wasn't quite ready for a wedding. They both started at once.

They laughed.

"You first," Evan insisted.

Sky took a deep breath and prayed a quick prayer. "Mr...? I'm sorry, I don't know your name."

"Trent, Evan Trent. I guess I don't know yours either."

"Sky Hoffman." She smiled briefly. "Mr. Trent—"

"Evan, please."

In her upbringing it was highly improper to use first names, but Sky nodded, impatient to get this over with. "Evan. Would you mind...would you...could we...wait... awhile before we—"

Evan sighed with relief.

"You mean, could we wait about getting married?"

She nodded.

"Yes."

He smiled wider. "I don't mean to sound so relieved, Miss Hoffman, but that was going to be my suggestion too. I've made arrangements for you to stay at the doctor's house because he and his wife are friends of mine. Would that be acceptable to you?"

Sky breathed a thankful prayer. "Yes, I would very much like that." The man was so thoughtful! Perhaps things would work out after all. "Would you mind if first I attended the wedding of my friend Miranda?"

"Not at all. Was she the one kidnapped by the Indians?"

"Yes, and I was the other one. We were rescued by Hank Riley, that's the man Randi is marrying, and by... Russ Newly." Sky said the name softly.

Evan was curious at the change in her voice when she said the man's name.

They joined Randi and Hank, and Sky introduced them. The women excused themselves so Randi could get ready.

Sky helped Randi into one of her own dresses for her wedding, and she insisted on giving her friend several outfits as a wedding gift despite her protests.

Randi questioned Sky about Evan.

"He's very nice. I like him," she told Randi. She explained about staying at the doctor's.

"You haven't forgotten Russ already, have you?" asked Randi.

"No, I don't think I'll ever forget him, but I can't just sit here in this town waiting for him. He never said anything about coming for me, you know." Although she kept her voice matter-of-fact, inwardly Sky was overcome with confusion. She had no doubt of her love for Russ, but not knowing how he felt about her was leaving her little choice but to fulfill her contract to marry Evan Trent. She was running out of time. If only she knew what to do.

"Well, keep praying, Sky. The LORD will show you."

The wedding was simple and beautiful. Randi was radiant, and Hank's love glowed in his eyes.

Sky hugged Randi close. Her heart felt happiness and heaviness at the same time. She was going to miss this "sister" she had found.

Hank hugged her next. "You take good care of her, Mr. Hank-Hector-Riley!" she scolded. He squeezed her arm and smiled.

"I will. You take care too. Russ told me to make sure you'd be okay. Will you?"

She nodded, not daring to speak.

The parlor door opened, and Angelina and Becky came in with a very different-looking Duke Tunelle. He had coerced the barber into postponing his own wedding to shave him and cut his hair. Sky was startled by his handsome appearance, and Angelina was obviously pleased.

The weddings continued, but Evan and Sky stepped back outside to join Hank and Randi for supper. Afterwards they headed back down the boardwalk. A gust of wind blew at the women's skirts, and the men grabbed for their hats.

"Storm's blowing in," said Evan. "Looks to be a bad one."

Hank looked at the blackening sky and turned to Randi. "How about if we stay in town tonight and start out in the morning?"

She smiled back and agreed with him that that would be best.

"There is no hotel yet in the town," Evan started to explain.

"That's okay," said Hank. "How about that old covered wagon you and Sky shared? Think it could keep us dry for one more night?"

Again Randi smiled, and Sky laughed. Randi would probably agree to anything this new husband of hers suggested.

They walked to the edge of town where the wagons were, but were stopped when a voice hailed them. Sky's heart sank as she saw Rudolph Hadley step briskly toward them. Evan, noticing her look, eyed the man with suspicion. This was the man who had been asking questions around town.

"Miss Hoffman, I was hoping to have a word with you and with this gentleman as well." He pointed to Evan.

"You have nothing to say that we want to hear," began Sky. She spoke loudly over the wind.

"Oh but I do, Sky. It is only fair to the man to let him know that I have prior legal claim to you." He took papers from inside his coat and spread them open for Evan to see and started explaining the situation.

Sky groaned and turned away, exasperated with the man; then she turned back curiously as she saw Hank walk over and stand between the men.

"Getting dark with all these clouds!" he shouted. "Here, let me help."

With a side glance and a wink at the women, he took a match from his vest pocket and struck it. He held it close to the papers so that Evan could see them better; then, to Sky and Randi's horror and delight, he started the papers on fire.

"Oh! I'm terribly sorry!" He grabbed the papers and shook them in the wind, and as a furious Hadley reached for them, he fumbled and let them go.

"You fool!" Hadley shouted. His face was red with rage.

The papers swirled away in the gusty wind. Red and black ashes scattered as they disintegrated into the darkening sky.

Hadley spun back to confront Hank with a raised fist, but Hank innocently reached out to extend a repentant hand and knocked Hadley off the boardwalk into the dirt street.

With many an apology, he and Evan helped the sputtering Englishman to his feet. He shook free of them and pointed to Sky.

"This won't stop me, Sky!" He straightened his coat and left.

Chapter 27

Sand Creek

Evan paced the now empty parlor, trying to digest what Sky had told him about Rudolph Hadley. He believed her, and he wanted to help her. But how? The English gent had money, and it didn't look like he was going to give up easily. On the other hand, this was a way to get out of his obligation. He quickly dismissed that thought. He couldn't do that to Sky. Though he had only known her for a day, he already cared about her happiness.

Sky quietly watched him. Again she was dependent on others to help her, and she hated it. All she wanted was to find her sister. She sighed.

"I'm sorry, Sky; you must be exhausted. Why don't I go home so you can get to bed? We'll have to pray the LORD shows us what to do."

Sky was pleased to hear him talk about the LORD. What a nice man he was! She yawned. She was tired! She stood and murmured, "All I wanted was to find my sister."

"What sister?"

Sky yawned again. "I'm looking for my twin sister. Hadley tells me his detectives can't find her." Her sleepiness made her feel silly, and she giggled. "Do you know anyone who looks like me?"

"Ella does," Evan answered without thinking.

"Who's Ella?"

"Well, she's...she works with the doc, and she stays here usually. She's...kind of...a, a friend of mine," he stammered.

Sky's sleepiness vanished. She wasn't aware of Evan's discomfort; she only heard that Ella looked like her. "Where is she? When can I see her? Describe her for me."

Evan put his hands up to stop her questions. "Wait now, Sky. She may not be who you're looking for. I just thought when I first saw you that you reminded me of Ella. Ella Burkett is her full name." He explained about Michael.

"But what does she look like?" Sky was insistent.

"Well..." He scratched his head. "She's real pretty. She's about the same size as you and her hair is blonde too. Her eyes are blue, but they're darker than yours. Let's see...I don't know what else to tell you."

"She wouldn't have to look exactly like me, would she? She could be the one! Oh, Evan! I have to see her and talk to her. When?"

Evan was getting more and more uncomfortable. He hadn't wanted Sky and Ella to meet until he had settled Sky with someone else, but this was so important to her that he found himself saying,

"I guess I could take you out to the Widow Poole's tomorrow, if you feel up to it."

"I'll be ready first thing in the morning. Oh thank you, Evan! You don't know how much this means to me." She threw her arms around the startled man and gave him a quick hug.

Embarrassed, Evan backed out of the room, nearly tripping over the rocker.

"I'll see you tomorrow, then, Sky. Good night."

Sky's eyes were dreamy as she laid down for the night. Tomorrow she just might meet her very own sister! Maybe that's why God put her on that wagon train. And Evan was nice. She felt she could learn to get along with him, maybe even marry him after all. She forced herself to push thoughts of Russ back into the recesses of her mind.

Evan's thoughts were in a turmoil as he rode for home. The storm had brought rain, thunder, and lightening, but it was nothing compared to his inner distress.

Tomorrow he was going to introduce the girl he was in love with to the girl he was supposed to be engaged to. He must be crazy!

Sky sat nervously beside Evan in the buggy. She was trying to pay attention as he pointed out places and points of interest on their way, but her mind was on Ella Burkett.

Evan noticed her preoccupation. "Sky, she may not be the person you're looking for. I'm sorry now that I even said anything." He silently rebuked himself for getting into this mess.

"I know, Evan. I keep telling myself that too, but I just feel that today...something is going to change for me, something is going to happen. Do you know what I mean? Have you ever felt that way?" Sky twisted the bag in her hands as she chattered on and on.

"My mother used to have feelings like that too. It would drive the baron crazy, and you know, I think she sometimes did it on purpose. She—"

"The baron?"

"My stepfather. Mother took me to England when I was a baby, and she married the baron. She really had no choice, you see, because her sister, Elaine, made her do it. That's when I lost my twin sister, see? Elaine sent *her* away on a wagon train."

The buggy pulled to a stop in front of a small cabin. Instead of getting down, Evan just sat staring curiously at Sky for a few moments while she nervously patted her hair and glanced around her.

Did she really say Elaine?

He was about to question Sky, but the door opened and a young woman stepped out on the porch. Evan turned away from Sky and saw Ella. She appeared very surprised and not at all pleased, but she composed herself quickly and waited patiently for them to descend from the buggy.

Evan looked from one woman to the other and shook his head. Why did he think they looked alike? There were similarities, true, but not enough to have warranted this trip out here. Events were moving too quickly, but he knew God had a hand in this. And only God was going to be able to sort out this twisted, mixed-up, bizarre situation the three of them were now in. For the moment all he could do was watch.

Ella was becoming embarrassed by the silence and the way the beautiful woman with Evan was staring at her. Evan saw her dart an angry glance his way and knew she wondered why he had brought Sky here.

"Miss Ella Burkett, I would like you to meet Miss Sky Hoffman. Miss Hoffman, Miss Burkett." Evan made the introduction then waited in silence.

Sky stood where she was and continued to stare at Ella. Ella looked again to Evan, but getting no help from him, she finally stepped from the porch and held out her hand to Sky.

"How do you do, Miss Hoffman?"

Sky took the outstretched hand and held on to it. Ella finally noticed the anticipation in Sky's eyes and asked, "Is there something wrong?"

Sky started to speak, cleared her throat, and tried again. Finally she blurted, "How old are you?"

Ella was taken aback, and Evan smiled behind his hand as he rubbed his chin.

"Why do you—?"

"Please, I'm sorry. I didn't mean to offend you, Miss Burkett." Sky had turned pink with embarrassment. "You see, I'm looking for my twin sister who was sent to this state on a wagon train twenty years ago when she was a newborn baby." She waited with a dry-mouth.

Ella was perplexed, and she just looked at the English woman strangely.

Evan took pity on her although he was amused at the way the two women were staring at each other. Sky's look was hopeful and Ella's was suspicious. "I think Miss Hoffman believes you could be her twin sister, Ella."

Ella looked from him back to Sky. "But why me? What made you think I could be related to you?"

"Well, you are the same size, and you do have the same color of hair." Evan was enjoying himself. In fact, he had never felt better. In all his worrying and praying and wondering what to do about his contracted bride and his love for Ella, he never dreamed of an answer like this one. *Only you, God!* He thought. *Only you could have done this.*

Ella scowled when she saw that Evan was amused. She spoke carefully to Sky. "I don't think I am the person you are looking for, Miss Hoffman. I was born and raised out west. I'm one of seven children, and I'm...I'm twenty-two years old." She glanced quickly at Evan, who raised his eyebrows, then back to Sky again. "I am sorry."

Sky's shoulders slumped and she let out a sigh. "I'm sorry to have bothered you, Miss Burkett. I just hoped—"

Evan cleared his throat. "Well, we tried, Sky. Are you done here yet, Ella?"

Ella now turned her astonished expression back to Evan. "Mrs. Poole has recovered well enough," she answered cautiously.

"Great! Then why not gather your things, and Sky and I will take you back to town with us."

Stunned and with a little hurt in her eyes, Ella started to protest, but Sky forestalled her.

"Please do, Miss Burkett, I would like to get to know you even if you aren't my twin." She smiled her charming smile. "I guess we can share the room at the doctor's until I...until we..." She looked uncomfortably at Evan as she stammered to a stop, and her embarrassment was evident in the pink that returned to her cheeks.

"Well, that will be fine, then, won't it. Go along and get your things, and I'll load them here in back." Evan suppressed the desire to laugh at Ella's expression.

They started back in silence. Ella was stiff-backed on the seat beside Sky, who sat beside Evan. Evan had offered to let Ella sit on the other side of him, but she had politely refused.

Evan was fairly sure he could guess at the thoughts of his traveling companions. Sky was obviously disappointed in Ella not being her twin. From her furtive glances his way, he surmised she was worried about having to marry him. Seemed to him that she had an interest in that Newly fellow she mentioned. That would be good.

He refrained from letting his smile show as he glimpsed Ella on the other side of Sky. She absolutely refused to look his way, staring straight ahead. He could only hope she would forgive him for what he was about to do.

Evan broke the silence.

"I just had an idea. Since we're this close, how would you ladies like to see my homestead?"

Sky wasn't sure she was ready to deal with that yet, but she gave Evan a brief smile and nodded. Ella made a choking sound and refused to look at him.

His land wasn't far, and before long Evan pulled the horses to a stop in front of a neat log cabin. The women looked at it curiously, noting the wash pan and towel hanging on the outside wall. The sun shone on a dusty, curtainless window, but the overall appearance was neat and showed care.

"It isn't much yet, but I have plans to add on more in the future, especially as my family grows." Evan helped the ladies down and pretended not to notice that they both avoided looking at him.

"Over there is the barn and corral. There's the well, and I'm starting to plow a garden spot right over there."

They followed his arm as he pointed at the sites. Ella stood stiffly behind Sky. Her cheeks had hot angry flames in them, and she dropped her eyes whenever Evan looked her way. He decided his teasing had gone on long enough.

"Come inside, and I'll fix you something cool to drink. There's something I'd like to show you, both of you." He caught and held Ella's eyes.

Sky was finally beginning to notice the tension between Evan and Ella. She realized that while she had been dwelling on her own problems, Ella had not spoken since they left the Widow Poole's. She looked at her curiously as they entered the cabin.

"Please sit down. I'll be right back." Evan left, and the women again let their eyes study the home of this man.

Everything was neat and clean but definitely the home of a bachelor.

I'd put up curtains and use a matching tablecloth, thought Sky. *He needs more shelves too, no, cupboards would be nicer.*

She noticed a Bible lying open on the table, so she walked over to it and let her finger run down the words in the book of Proverbs until it came to some that had been underlined. She read out loud from chapter three, verses five and six, "Trust in the LORD with all thine heart; and lean not unto thine own understanding. In all thy ways acknowledge him, and he shall direct thy paths."

Sky looked up at Evan, who was walking in with a pitcher in his hands. She spoke to both him and Ella, and her voice was filled with wonder. "I hadn't read that before. I haven't known the LORD very long, but to know that he wants to direct my path means so much to me. Sometimes I feel like I don't know where I'm headed or what's going to happen next, but now I know. The LORD will direct me. Isn't that wonderful?"

Ella sat down in the chair facing the open Bible. "I guess I forget that sometimes," she said softly. She looked at Evan and then dropped her eyes again.

"It is a wonderful promise, Sky." Evan poured cold water for his guests and set it before them. "When we acknowledge the LORD, when we ask his help, he gladly directs us. I think the hard part is letting him. 'Trust in the LORD with all thine heart.' Sometimes we just don't trust him to work things out in our lives." He smiled. "But he does. Will you wait here a moment, please?"

Again Evan left the room, but this time he went to a room off the kitchen. Sky glimpsed a bed before the door closed behind him.

"He's a nice man, isn't he?" Sky asked Ella.

"Yes...he's been very helpful to me." Ella became quiet again, and Sky remained silent until Evan returned.

He held an envelope in his hand and had a big smile on his face. "Sorry I took so long, but I wanted to read this one more time just to be sure. Ella, would you read this note out loud for us?" Evan handed the envelope to Ella; then he fastened his eyes on Sky.

Ella reluctantly took the worn paper and opened the note. She was aware of Evan's interest in Sky, and in a flat voice she began to read:

Dear Wee Babe,

I didn't want to take you from your pretty little mother and sister. Mrs. Elaine made me do it. That woman is evil. The hardest thing I ever did was to wrap you up and hand you over to another family, but they look to be a good family. I pray all will work out for you, and, Lord willing, that you find your Ma and sister again. They're sending them to England, so maybe you won't.

Your Ma's name is Lucille. I was her midwife who delivered you.

"It's signed Fay O'Brian," Ella finished. In puzzlement, she looked up to see Sky's eyes filled with tears as she stared at Evan.

Evan spoke. "I was told the note was brought to the wagon train just before it left. My mother and father gave it to me as soon as they felt I was old enough to understand."

"*You're* my twin! My twin *brother!* But how can that be? My mother said I had a twin sister." Uncertainty crossed Sky's face.

"Do you remember exactly what your mother said?" Evan's voice was quiet but confident.

"I have it here; I carry it with me." Sky fumbled in the small bag on her wrist. She handed Evan the letter from her mother and watched breathlessly while he read. *A brother?*

Sky studied Evan's bent head as he carefully read through the letter. "Yes! Don't you see, Sky? Our mother only held us briefly before she went to sleep. No one told her one baby was a girl and one was a boy, so she assumed they were both girls. She assumed it because they were twins! And Elaine let her think so."

"Oh, Evan! Have I found my twin at last?" Sky stepped up to him and placed a hand on his cheek. She studied his face carefully.

"Of course I'm not as pretty as you are." Evan grinned. "But look at us. Both blond, blue eyes, same noses—"

"Same chin, same voice inflections, same smile," Ella continued the comparison while she slowly rose to her feet. "So that's why you brought us here."

Evan looked at Ella, and Sky saw love in his expression. A sudden thought made her exclaim, "My goodness, Evan! I was going to marry you!"

They all laughed, and Evan held his arms out to Sky. "Welcome home, sister!" Sky embraced her twin brother with tears of joy flowing from her eyes.

"God directed our paths, didn't he!"

"He surely did." They looked at each other and hugged again. Then Evan held Sky at arm's length and said, "I know we have a lot to talk about, but before we get started, I would like to know how you feel about having a real sister too."

As Sky smiled, he held out his hand to Ella and said, "Now will you marry me?"

In a moment Ella was in his arms. Sky was delighted. She clapped her hands like a little girl receiving a new toy. Evan was sure of her approval.

He held Ella close and whispered in a teasing voice, "So my bride is two years older than me. I think I like it."

"You'd better like it!"

Chapter 28

Sand Creek

"But do you think it will work?"

"Sky, we have to do something fast or Rudolph Hadley will never leave you alone."

Evan sat in the doctor's parlor, Ella by his side. Sky was facing him.

Gretchen and Bridget and the doctor and Florrie stood in the room as well. The newly married sisters had come the next day to tell Sky that Hadley had sent one of the detectives for the nearest lawman to enforce his legal rights to Sky.

The group pondered over the problem until Sky had muttered, "Russ said the only way to get Hadley to leave me alone was to get married."

Evan stared at his sister a moment and then exclaimed, "That's it, Sky!"

"What?"

"We can make Hadley think you got married."

Sky shook her head, not understanding, and the others looked just as perplexed.

"You know how I said you and Ella looked alike?"

Sky nodded, glancing at Ella, who seemed just as puzzled as she was.

"Let's make him think Ella is you when she and I get married."

The others thought about it awhile, and Ella was the first to agree. "I could wear a veil so he couldn't see me closely."

"And it would have to be a real ceremony, or he would be suspicious," said Evan.

"But then I won't be able to be at the wedding too," was all Sky could think of.

"Sky," said Gretchen, "it's wonderful that you've found your twin brother and all, but you'll have to do this quickly before the whole community finds out, or this wedding will never work. You don't want Rudolph Hadley pestering you *and* your brother, do you?"

Sky shook her head. "I still don't know why that man is interested in me. Everyone in England knew the baron left me no money."

"I'm pretty sure I know why he wants you," said Evan angrily, "and that's exactly why I won't let him have you. This will work, Sky."

"And you can watch the whole wedding from the kitchen," said Florrie. "No one will ever see you."

Sky still wasn't sure. "Isn't it really lying?"

"I don't intend to lie at all," said Evan. "He can believe what he wants. I think it will work. If he believes you're already married, he no longer has 'legal' claim to you, if he ever did."

Sky sat in silence while the others looked on and waited for her decision. The announcement that Evan was her twin had amazed them all, but now that they knew, they could see the resemblances, and soon everyone else would too. If this wedding was to work, it had to be done with all haste.

"If Ella doesn't mind a wedding where everyone thinks she's me, then...okay," Sky agreed.

Evan and Ella finally sat alone in the doctor's parlor. Ella noticed absently that Florrie's tastes in color ran to the deep shades of plum and navy as evidenced by the horse-hair sofa and chairs. The wooden rocker held a flowered pillow in the same hues, which also matched the drapes at the window. She realized suddenly that as her eyes had been roaming the contents of the room, Evan's had remained intent on her. There was something in the way he was looking at her that made her feel breathless. She cleared her throat.

"It's really wonderful about you and Sky," she opened the conversation.

"Ella."

She turned to look up at him.

Evan placed his hand over hers while he held her eyes. "Ella, I've just realized that I've railroaded you into a wedding before I even checked with you about your wishes. It *is* wonderful about finding Sky, and I want to help her with this Hadley fellow, but I should have spoken with you first before I concocted this wedding plan."

Evan shushed Ella's protests as he continued. "You are going to be my wife, and I should have put your considerations first. I'm sorry."

Evan paused and watched surprise cross Ella's features. Again he felt bad for not considering her feelings before blurting out his suggestions. He knew the plan could work to help Sky, but if he hurt his bride's feelings in the process, it would be the wrong thing to do.

When Ella didn't speak, Evan tried to explain. "Ella, I grew up in a family where my folks weren't afraid to show me that they loved each other. Their example of putting the other first has always been one I wanted to follow. I want to make you happy, Ella."

Silent tears slid down Ella's face, and Evan was torn inside when he saw them. "Obviously I'm not doing a very good job of it," he whispered as he gently wiped them away.

Ella suddenly laughed then smiled at Evan's confused look. "Oh, Evan! You have no idea how special your words are to me."

"I told you I was raised in a family of seven children. Well, I'm the youngest of the seven, and as my brothers and sisters kept marrying off and leaving the farm, I was left with more and more of the chores to do." Ella sniffed and accepted Evan's handkerchief. She wiped the remaining tears while he waited for her to continue.

"Then my parents died of influenza when I was sixteen," she went on. "I was left at home with two brothers and one sister. My sister soon married and left the farm, and I had all the house chores to do alone, plus the milking and the chickens to care for. My brothers both eventually married and split the farm between the two of them. My brother Kendall built a house on the far corner of the property, and that left the farmhouse to my brother James.

"Suddenly I was out of a place to live. James's new wife didn't want me living with them, so I had to leave and find work in town, which I did at the doctor's office. I was given no choice in the matter. It's been that way all my life."

Evan listened closely to his bride's words and realized that there was a lot she didn't say—a lot of sorrow and hurt that had never healed.

"The doctor retired from his practice several months ago, and the new young doctor's wife didn't want me helping her husband. I was out of a job and a place to live again. That's why I answered Michael Calloway's ad for a bride and why I decided to come to Sand Creek." Ella finished her story and waited for Evan's reaction. The question she had been expecting was not long in coming.

"Why didn't you marry someone from your town? At twenty-two you must have had several offers."

Ella sighed. "There were offers," she admitted.

"With each one I felt that he wanted another hired hand for his farm, not a wife to love and cherish, just as most of the men wanted who asked me to marry them here in Sand Creek. Michael's letters were different. I felt he was looking for a companion, not just someone to do the chores."

Ella took a deep breath before continuing. "And I feel that way with you, Evan. I've come to love you. I know there will be work on your farm, and I'm not afraid of that. That was never the issue. I know that you care about me; you just proved that again with your apology. You have no idea how good it feels to know someone wants to take care of me."

Evan pulled Ella into his arms and held her close. *How could anyone not love and cherish this special woman?* he thought. Aloud, he began to pray, "LORD, help me be the husband Ella needs me to be. I pray that our marriage will honor you and reflect your love." He finished with a plea on Sky's behalf and then looked down into his beloved's face.

Ella's eyes sparkled with tears that clung to her lashes. "Evan, thank you for asking me about the wedding. I'm truly fine with the plan to help Sky, and I'm so very thankful to be getting a husband who cares about me the way that you do."

"You haven't seen anything yet," promised Evan.

Rudolph Hadley and his man Smythe walked down the boardwalk to Nolan's mercantile. The Englishman's fancy black suit was out of place in the primitive frontier community.

"I shall be happy to return to a civilized way of life," commented Hadley.

"Yes, sir," agreed Smythe heartily.

They stepped into the store, and Smythe began to shop for the items his employer requested while Hadley stood in the doorway and looked out at the street. He watched Sky step from the doctor's home and walk to the blacksmith's home to speak to the woman there. She must have had good news, for the women embraced; then Sky hurried back and entered the doctor's home again. Hadley scowled. He planned to talk to her today if she would stay there. She had been spending too much time with that Trent fellow to suit him. He wanted to convince her that according to his detectives, her twin sister was dead. Maybe that would make her more willing to leave here. His thoughts were interrupted as he became aware of the women talking in the store.

"Yes, it's true. Evan Trent finally decided to tie the knot. He was a bit bashful at first. Why look, the rest of us are all married already except for Sky."

"I hear she's delighted about the whole thing. She's really come to love Evan."

"And they're getting married right now. Just think! We all made happy marriages."

The talk went on, but Hadley stopped listening. He saw the blacksmith's wife scurry to the doctor's home in a fancy dress. And he saw the preacher step down from his horse and enter right after her. *She wouldn't dare!*

"Smythe!" Hadley strode from the store and down the boardwalk, and his man hurried after him after dropping his purchases on the counter. Gretchen and Bridget stopped their chatter and looked after the hurrying men.

Hadley reached the doctor's home with Smythe still trying to catch up to him. He slammed open the gate and marched up to the house and entered without knocking. A man and a woman stood in front of the preacher. The man was dressed in a suit, and the woman wore a white dress and a veil covered her head. A blonde braid hung down her back.

The preacher kept speaking though the doctor, Florrie, and Belle turned at Hadley's intrusion.

"And do you, Evan, take this woman whom you hold by the hand to be your lawfully wedded wife?"

"I do." Evan spoke the words clearly.

"No!" shouted Hadley.

The preacher kept talking as he had been instructed. "...pronounce you husband and wife. You may kiss the bride."

Evan lifted Ella's veil partway and gently kissed her. Then he turned to an outraged Hadley and said in a stern voice, "Hadley, you will leave my wife alone from now on. Your 'legal claim' is voided, and should you even dare speak to my wife, you will have to deal with me."

The Englishman stared at the younger man. He was furious. "Don't think you've heard the last from me!"

"We have! That lawman you sent for will uphold the law here. This is *my* wife. This *is* the end, Hadley."

The angry man spun on his heel and left. Smythe caught up with him down the street. "I could make her a widow, sir, if you wish." The evil glint in his eye indicated he would enjoy doing so.

"No. I'm tired of the chase, Smythe. There are others with more wealth than Sky Hoffman. I think it is time to move on. I'm glad for the excuse to get out of this miserable country. She deserves to stay here."

Sky cautiously came out of the kitchen and looked at the group still staring after Hadley.

"Is he gone?" she asked quietly.

"Gone for good, I'd say," announced the doctor. "Now how about some celebrating! I've lost one assistant and gained a new one." He smiled at Sky.

"And I've gained not only a brother but a sister as well." She embraced her newfound family.

Ella threw back the veil and smiled as Sky hugged her. "I wish you'd come stay with us, Sky. We'd love to have you."

Evan agreed. "There's room at our homestead, Sky. We should be like a family for a while."

Sky smiled and shook her head at the newlyweds. "I'll be out there so much you'll think I live there. But no, I want to work here with the doctor and earn my way. Remember, the LORD will direct my paths. He's been doing a wonderful job so far."

"What about Russ Newly?" Belle asked Sky quietly. Ella and Evan looked curiously at their sister.

"I guess the LORD hasn't directed me down that path," answered Sky soberly.

Chapter 29

Sand Creek

"I was so relieved to hear that Hadley left town for good. And it's simply amazing that your twin sister turned out to be a brother right here in Sand Creek." Martha Riggs visited with Sky in the doctor's parlor. Her children played quietly on the floor beside the women.

"The LORD has been amazing me ever since I met him," agreed Sky. "How are you and Jasper getting along?"

"He's a quiet man, but he loves the children. I'm so thankful for that. And he's good to me too. We're still getting to know each other, almost courting even though we're married. I think this will work out fine." Martha sighed and tucked a curl behind her ear. "I don't think Violet is very pleased, though."

"She married that tall man, didn't she? He was very handsome. I remember that she grabbed his picture from my hands. Why, what's wrong?"

"I think Taylor likes having a pretty wife just like he likes a fancy buggy and horse. He's all show. Violet is really just a showpiece, not a companion. I think she's lonely."

Sky felt sorry for Violet even though the young woman had never been kind to her. She wondered if Violet would be willing to be friends now. "How are Angelina and Becky?" she asked next.

"Sky, they are so happy! I can't believe the changes in Duke Tunelle. The men here say he's like his old self, the way he was before the Indian raid. And he is caring for Angelina as if she's a special treasure. They were both in town a couple of days ago shopping for the new baby."

"Oh, I'm sorry I missed them. The doctor keeps me pretty busy, so I'm gone a lot, but I really enjoy helping him. And Janet Conly, I mean Janet Spencer, is her husband still afraid of her?" Sky asked with a giggle.

Martha joined in her laughter. "He was, but I think he's really quite proud of Janet. He was a quiet man that no one noticed before; now everyone knows when they're in town."

"And you, Sky? Are you still getting proposals?" Martha laughed at Sky's expression.

"Unfortunately, yes. I think they will taper off soon; I mean, really, there can't be that many men left around here. I don't know how Ella could put up with it."

"None of them suit you?"

Sky laughed. "Now don't you start!"

Martha picked up her baby and checked the diaper. "Are you waiting for someone in particular?" She looked sideways at her friend.

"I'm waiting. I have this feeling that I should wait." She looked intently at Martha. "I'm not saying that I'm waiting for Russ. I don't know if he's the man the LORD has for me or not, but I know the LORD will show me when the time is right. He's been doing a pretty good job so far."

Sky was gone visiting at Evan and Ella's home when Russ Newly rode into town. It had taken a long time to round up the gang down south. Then he had to make his reports and request time for this trip. His boss was reluctant to give him the free time, but Russ was adamant.

Now he wondered, as he sat looking around him, if it had been a wise thing to do. Sky might already be married. He never got the chance to ask her to wait for him. But he had to come. He couldn't think of anything else but her. He had to know.

As he tied his horse, he noticed another rider come down the dusty street into town. The man was struggling to keep his horse headed in the right direction and was riding like he had never been on horseback before. He was obviously a city man, dressed in a city suit and totally out of place in a town like Sand Creek. Russ watched him with curiosity then glanced around the small town. He spotted the mercantile and headed in that direction.

He didn't want his presence known until he knew more about Sky. The detective in him made him cautious, so he found a bench near the door to the store and sat down, stretching his long legs out in front of him. He tipped his hat down over his eyes and waited.

The mercantile was busy, and before long he heard women's voices that he thought he recognized from the wagon train. One was definitely one of the Irish girls, the O'Donnells, he recalled.

"Sure, and have you heard the good news about Sky and Evan Trent?"

"Yes, isn't it wonderful! I even attended the wedding. The bride was so beautiful. Sky is as happy as can be about the whole thing. And we're all glad Rudolph Hadley gave up and left. I was ready to have my Clyde send him packing."

Russ felt as though he had been punched in the stomach. He closed his eyes tightly at the pain the words brought him. He heard footsteps, and from under the brim of his hat he noticed the fancy rider entering the mercantile.

In his remorse over hearing that Sky was married, Russ paid no attention to what was being said until he heard Sky's name again.

"Miss Sky Hoffman of England?" The fancy gent was speaking.

"What do ye want with our Sky?"

"If you could just tell me how to reach her, I'd be much obliged, ladies. I have important legal matters to discuss with her."

"If you work for that Rudolph Hadley, you can just leave right now, mister."

"I know no one of that name. I am a lawyer from New York. I have been employed through a firm in London to handle the affairs of the estate of Miss Hoffman's late step-uncle. Now, if you can please tell me where she is?"

Russ listened closely. Finally he heard one of the women speak.

"She's probably at the Trent homestead now." And she gave the man directions.

Russ waited for the man to leave and was about to rise when the voices spoke again.

"I sure do hope this won't be bad news for Sky. She's been so happy lately."

"Hasn't she, though! Especially with the new baby coming and all. Sure, and she's in here all the time buying some little thing for it."

Russ felt his mouth go dry. He forced himself up and went to his horse. He would leave town. He would leave now before anyone recognized him and told Sky he had been there. She deserved the happiness she had found. He didn't want to spoil it for her.

He led his horse away from the town and started riding. His heart felt heavy, and his shoulders slumped. He should have spoken to her and let her know how he felt about her! Now it was too late.

"Lord, why did you let me come all the way here just to be disappointed?" Russ spoke the words in anger. In a flash, the answer came to him.

"*What time I am afraid, I will trust in thee.*"

The verse in the Psalms popped into Russ's head and shamed him for his thoughts. He stopped his horse. His anger left him.

You're right, Lord. I should trust you to lead the way. I guess this wasn't it, was it?

He sat deep in thought for a few moments then checked his surroundings. He was headed in the direction the woman gave to the Trent homestead. He would like to see for himself if Sky was truly happy or not. She wouldn't have to see him. He turned toward the homestead.

Russ spotted the fancy lawyer's horse in front of the small log cabin. It was a nice cabin, a nice location. The man Evan Trent was doing well for himself. He saw a man working in a garden near the house. *Must be him.* Russ squinted to get a better look at him. Nice enough looking fellow, he had to admit.

He waited, concealed in some trees, to catch a glimpse of Sky. He felt more at peace about it now. He wanted Sky to be happy.

Suddenly the door of the cabin flew open, and Sky came running out, waving a paper in her hand.

"Evan! Evan, look at this! We've inherited the money!" She ran to the man in the field.

Russ's heart pounded at the sight of her.

He saw Sky throw her arms around the bewildered man. Evan looked at the paper and said something to her; then he picked her up and swung her around in the air. They started back to the house with their arms around each other's waists.

Russ had seen enough. He tore his eyes from Sky's smiling face and walked his horse away from the farm.

Russ made camp that night with a heavy heart. He talked to the LORD more about his feelings.

Help me get over this, Lord. I love her still, but that's not right. She belongs to another.

He tossed on his bedroll, finding little comfort. He kept seeing Sky throw her arms around Evan, and each time it felt like a knife twist in his gut.

"Trust in the Lord with all thine heart."

The quiet thought came to him again. It was funny how God's Word came to his mind at times like this.

Okay, Lord. I do trust you. Lead me where you want me to go next.

He slept late the next morning. It had been a struggle most of the night until he had given himself over to the LORD's leading again. Russ felt peaceful, though an emptiness remained.

He saddled up and began to ride. He would head for the nearest town with a telegraph and get new orders from his boss. He felt a desperate need to be busy.

The sunlight warmed his shoulders and sparkled through the trees. He thought of how the sun shone on Sky's golden hair and how her smile echoed its brilliance. Forgetting her wasn't going to be easy.

A shot up ahead startled him out of his musings. His gun appeared in his hand in a flash, and his eyes searched for the location of the gunman.

Another shot spurred Russ to action. He rode into a nearby grove of trees and tethered his horse. He crouched down and crept forward to get a better view. Peering through the trees, Russ could see a wounded man propped behind a rock, trying to defend himself against his attackers. Russ judged there to be two men shooting at him.

He sized up the situation before acting. The man's left arm was hanging limply at his side, and Russ could see blood staining the sleeve. He was struggling to reload his rifle with the one good arm. As more shots rained down on the man, Russ made his move.

He fired a shot first at one attacker and then the other before he rolled and ran to a new position. As he had hoped, the men turned their attack on him, giving the wounded man the chance that he needed to reload.

The shots continued to slice through the morning air as Russ raced to a better position and was finally able to see the attackers.

Smythe! Hadley's man. What is he doing here? The women in town said Hadley had gone.

Russ aimed carefully and squeezed off his shot. He saw Smythe twist as the bullet hit him; then he lay still.

The wounded man had also stopped shooting. Russ hoped he wasn't dead. He waited, his knees pressed into the dirt, for Hadley to make the next move.

"Smythe! Smythe, answer me!" Russ heard Hadley's desperate whisper.

"He's dead, Hadley. And so will you be if you don't put down your gun right now. I've got a clear shot to your head, and I won't miss.

Hadley hesitated then dropped his gun.

"Get your hands where I can see them and walk over here."

Hadley stood and walked with his hands raised in the air to Russ. His eyes narrowed as he recognized the man.

"So we meet again, Hadley. Seems to me you're always causing trouble to someone."

"If you've come for another chance to win Sky Hoffman, you're too late, cowboy! She's mine! She and all the money are mine! Not even her marriage can stop me. And certainly you can't stop me," raved Hadley.

"Hadley, you've worn out your welcome in this country. The law will have to put a stop to you since you think nothing else can. Now shut up and hold out your hands."

Rudolph Hadley glared at Russ but said nothing more. Russ tied his hands and made him sit while he checked on the wounded man. He knew Smythe was dead.

Russ ran to where the man had been and called out, "Hold your fire, friend; I've come to help."

There was no answer as he rounded the corner. The man was slumped over in a heap.

Russ felt for a heartbeat as he turned the unconscious man onto his back. He checked the wound then looked into the man's face.

It was Evan Trent.

Chapter 30

Sand Creek

The odd procession caused quite a stir when it rode into Sand Creek.

Russ led the way, his arm snaked around Evan, holding him onto the saddle as they rode double on his horse. By Evan's slumped over position it was evident that he was unconscious. A rope tied to the saddle horn kept the three horses in line behind them. One held the body of Smythe tied over the saddle, one was empty, and the other held Hadley, tied hand and foot to his horse. The Englishman bore no resemblance now to being a gentleman. He glared angrily at the townspeople who gawked at him in his defeat.

The Nolan brothers ran to Russ first.

"What happened? Why, it's Evan Trent! Is he dead?"

"Where did Hadley come from? Why is he back here? Who are you, mister?"

"Do you gentlemen know where I can find a sheriff, a doctor, and an undertaker?" Russ asked.

The brothers took hold of the horses' heads. "The sheriff is here in town," announced Harry. He looked at Hadley. "In fact, Hadley's the one who sent for him in the first place. What happened?"

"Give this man over to the sheriff and have him charged with attempted murder."

"Attempted murder?"

Russ handed the rope on Hadley's horse to Harry. "Now, how about that doctor?"

Clyde Moore, the blacksmith, reached up to help Russ with Evan. "This is his house right here. Let me give you a hand."

The men carried Evan into the doctor's home. Russ saw two women rush to help them, and he faltered a step when he realized that one was Sky, her face ashen at seeing Evan injured. Russ was startled to find her there and totally unprepared to see her face-to-face.

Sky only saw Evan's crumpled form and paid no heed to the men who were carrying him. She cried, "Evan! Evan, my dear, are you all right? Evan, speak to me!"

The doctor pulled her aside and handed her to the other woman. "Let me have a look, Sky. Hold her there a moment, Florrie. Everything will be fine."

Russ's heart wrenched at Sky's distress. He couldn't seem to stop himself and spoke up. "I think he'll be okay. He took a bullet to the shoulder, and he's lost a lot of blood."

Sky jerked her head around at his voice. Her face registered shock at the sight of him. "Russ?"

The way she said his name and the way she looked at him made Russ's heart pound, but he kept a careful guard on his expression. They stared at each other until a man knocked and entered the room. It was the sheriff.

"Young man, if you're through here I'd like to ask you some questions about all this."

"Certainly, sheriff." Russ looked back at Sky who was still staring at him. "He'll be fine, Sky. Please don't worry."

The two men left, and Sky stared at the door. *Russ is here!* A moan from Evan made her turn her attention back to her wounded brother. She moved into a position to help the doctor as he had taught her. Her thoughts of Russ would have to wait.

Evan was resting comfortably at last. The doctor had given him something to ease the pain as he tended the wound. Before he slept again, Evan had told Sky and the doctor about Hadley's ambush.

"I was riding to Spencer's to check on some cows he wanted to sell when I was shot from my horse. I crawled behind a rock and started shooting back, but I didn't do much good with one arm. I saw that stranger stop and help me, and that's all I remember. I guess Hadley knew about your inheritance before you did and was determined to make you a widow so he could still marry you himself."

"*Our* inheritance. I'm just glad you're all right, Evan dear. You rest now. Clyde Moore took a buggy out to get Ella. She'll be here soon."

Sky held Evan's hand until he fell asleep again. Her relief that he was going to be all right was great, and now her thoughts returned to Russ. Would he come back to the doctor's house to see her again? She decided she couldn't wait. Evan would sleep a good long while then Ella would be here. She had to see Russ.

Sky looked up and down the street of the small town but could see no sign of Russ. She hurried to Nolan's mercantile, where she found Gretchen at the counter.

"Have you seen Russ Newly, Gretchen?"

The woman answered Sky quickly. "He left. After he told the sheriff what had happened, he started to get on his horse. Bridget ran up to him and asked him if he was going to go see you, but he said he already had. Did he, Sky?"

He left! Sky stared at Gretchen. "He only saw me when he brought Evan in—oh no! Gretchen, he thinks Evan and I are...no! I have to catch him! Which way was he headed?"

Sky ran to the street, searching for a horse. Evan's horse had been tied to the rail until someone could care for it. In a flash, she mounted astride and, with skirts flying, raced out of town in the direction Gretchen had indicated.

Her thoughts raced along with her horse. How could she make him understand without throwing herself at him? She didn't even know if he had come to see her.

It wasn't long until she caught up to him. Russ turned at the sound of the running horse and waited when he saw her. Again, his expression was guarded.

Sky stopped the winded horse and sat breathing hard as she studied Russ's face. They both waited uneasily as the dust around them settled, and the silence was broken by the songs of the birds.

From somewhere she found some courage to ask, "Where were you going, Russ Newly? Were you going to leave without talking to me?" She watched his face carefully and saw him struggle to find words.

Finally he answered quietly, "You were pretty busy."

"Evan is resting now, thanks to you. You were right; he will be fine. Why did you come to Sand Creek?" she demanded. She was surprised at her own boldness, but she had to know before he was gone forever.

"I came to see if you were happy, and I found that you were, so now I'm moving on."

There was barely a hint of unsteadiness in his voice, but Sky heard it.

Happiness and relief burst inside of her. She smiled.

"What if you found that I wasn't happy? What were you going to do about it?"

"Sky—"

"But you found that I was happy, so you were going to leave. Well, Russ, I am very happy."

He nodded and waited miserably.

Sky's pulse raced as she saw his expression. "In fact, did you know that I found my twin?"

He was surprised, and even through his pain, he was happy for her. "Sky, that's wonderful! Where was she? Who is she?"

"She turned out to be a *he*. A twin *brother*! And he was right here in Sand Creek. Can you guess his name?"

Russ's hands gripped the saddle horn. His eyes demanded her to continue.

She was breathless as she answered. "Evan Trent is my brother, Russ, not my husband."

He swung down from his horse and pulled her down into his arms.

Then he held her away and looked at her carefully. "Is there anyone else?"

She answered in a small voice, "Yes."

His hands began to fall, and she quickly added, "You!"

Russ pulled her to him roughly and held her so tightly Sky could scarcely breathe, but she didn't mind. This is what she had been waiting for; *he* was the one she had been wating for.

Russ's voice was muffled as he spoke, his face pressed against her golden hair. "What am I going to do with you, Sky? You know I love you? I never got the chance to tell you before I had to leave, but I haven't been able to stop thinking about you."

"I think maybe you should marry me, then, Mr. Newly. It would make sense, since I love you too, and I—"

Sky's words were cut off as Russ covered her mouth with his own.

Then he raised his head and he asked, "Will you marry me, Sky?"

Tears sparkled in her eyes, and she nodded, too emotional to speak her answer. The next moment Russ's Stetson was flying high into the air, and she was being twirled around and around.

A long while later, the two slowly rode back to Sand Creek.

"When I saw you run into Evan's arms at his homestead, I thought it was over, but God wouldn't let me leave. He kept leading me back."

"He led me all the way here from England, Russ. Now I know why. He led me to accept him; he led me to my brother; and he led me to you."

"I don't suppose you're too eager to leave your brother now that you've just found him and he and Ella are having their first baby. Do you think you'd like to settle here at Sand Creek?"

"What about your job?"

"I always said one day I would like a ranch of my own."

"The place next to Evan's is for sale. It belonged to a friend of his. Would that be all right?" She looked at him hopefully.

"We'll look at it today." Russ took one look at her happy face and smiled.

"And Hank and Randi said they'd be back too. Oh Russ, look how the LORD works everything out!"

He reached for her hand as they entered the town. People stepped out of doorways to watch them, and their friends began to rush toward them with smiling faces and laughter.

Sky was home.

For more information about
A Newly Weds Series or
author Margo Hansen, visit her at
www.margohansen.com.

Margo would enjoy hearing
from her readers. Send your
comments or questions to
margo@margohansen.com.